A WITCH FOR MR. GARLAND

WITCHES OF CHRISTMAS GROVE
BOOK SIX

DEANNA CHASE

ABOUT THIS BOOK

Welcome to Christmas Grove, the enchanting town full of love, magic, and holiday miracles.

Sixteen years ago, on a snowy December night, seer Danny Frost received a message from a mage that sent him running from the love of his life, Marissa Cane. Since then, Christmas has never been the same. But when Marissa unexpectedly walks back into his life, he's determined to right past wrongs and maybe find a way to heal both of their hearts.

Marissa Cane's heart was shattered at just nineteen, and since that day she stopped believing in fairy tales. So when a sugar plum fairy shows up in her adopted town of Christmas Grove with a message that could change everything, she's skeptical to say the least. But when an old curse rears its ugly head, the only way to keep her safe is to let Danny Frost back into her life. Now they need to work together to break the curse and to do that, they'll need a little holiday magic along the way.

CHAPTER 1

*M*arissa Cane flipped the Open sign around and unlocked the front door of Sleighed, the pub she'd owned for the past five years. She walked over to the bar, lit the candle on the cupcake, and smiled to herself as she blew it out. It was the pub's five-year anniversary, and she wanted to take a moment to herself to acknowledge everything that she'd accomplished since she'd moved to Christmas Grove.

Pride swelled in her chest as she looked at the framed photo of herself holding the keys the day she'd closed on the building. She was grinning and holding her arms out, so naive and unaware of what she was in for. And while it had been a rough couple of years in the beginning trying to keep the doors open, now her books were firmly in the black, and she was even starting to consider ways to expand.

The sound of a door slamming was followed quickly by her cook calling out, "I'm back!"

She walked over to the door that led to the kitchen and held it open, smiling at Jackson, the tall, handsome man who ran her kitchen. "Ready for a big night?"

"You know it!" He wrapped his apron around his waist and then waved at the refrigerator. "Everything has been prepped. Let the orders roll in."

"Great. Let's hope it's one for the books." The word had been put out that they were having an all-you-can-eat shrimp or crab night to celebrate the anniversary, and Marissa had invested a small fortune in bringing the shellfish over from the coast.

"I'm sure it will be. Who can resist fresh shrimp and crab?" The phone rang, and Jackson picked it up and answered. He immediately started scribbling down a phone order.

Marissa nodded at him and went back out into the pub just as the front door swung

open, and her two best friends swept inside carrying multiple bags and a pastry box.

"Happy anniversary!" Clara and Felicity cried together, both of them rushing over to the bar to unload their packages. Clara was a petite brunette whose smile lit up every room, and Felicity was a tall blonde with piercing blue eyes and was as loyal as they came. They were both a stark contrast to her fiery red hair and violet eyes.

"What did you two do?" Marissa asked as she watched Clara pick up the cupcake and shake her head.

The petite, raven-haired beauty made a face. "This

won't do. It won't do at all." She made a move to toss it into the trash.

"No!" Marissa lunged, but her friend moved it out of her reach. Narrowing her eyes, Marissa pierced Clara with her death glare. "That's a gingerbread cupcake from the Enchanted Bean Stalk. If you so much as harm one crumb, you'll regret it."

"Oh, will I?" Clara laughed her tinkling laugh as she opened up one of the boxes, revealing an unmistakable salted caramel chocolate cake from Love Potions, Christmas Grove's premier chocolate shop.

"Oh. Em. Gee." Marissa hurried behind the counter and grabbed a knife, ready to dive right into the sinful deliciousness. "I think I'm in love."

Felicity chuckled. "You're so predictable."

Marissa nodded. "It's true. Nothing is better than this cake. Nothing."

"Oh, I'd take a man who cooks. Preferably one with six-pack abs who likes to spend his time in the kitchen shirtless." Felicity flipped her long blond hair over her shoulder and then fanned herself with one hand.

"Why stop there?" Clara asked, grinning. "How about a house husband who likes to cook *and* clean?"

"Husband?" Felicity echoed, looking horrified. "Who said anything about a husband? The perfect guy is one who lives on the other side of town and comes over once a week to clean, prepare meals, and rumple the sheets."

Marissa and Felicity shared a glance and then started laughing. The both of them had the same feelings about marriage. Felicity had always maintained that getting married was an antiquated custom. Marissa just had no desire to go down that road again. Not that her friends even knew she'd been married once. It wasn't something she talked about. Ever.

Clara, on the other hand, still believed in the fairy tale.

"You two just wait," Clara said. "One day Mr. Perfect is going to walk into each of your lives, and suddenly you'll be singing a different tune."

Felicity rolled her eyes. "Doubtful."

Marissa just shook her head. There was no such thing as Mr. Perfect. She'd learned that the hard way.

"You two are far too cynical when it comes to matters of the heart," Clara said, pulling wrapped packages out of her shopping bags.

"What's all this?" Marissa asked, raising one eyebrow.

"We can't have a celebration without gifts," Clara said, giving Marissa a cheeky grin. "Now take a seat and get your gift on."

"What in the world?" Marissa sat heavily on a bar stool as she took in everything her friends had done. Her favorite cake and now gifts?

Clara started to pile them up on the bar while Felicity rubbed her hands together, eager for Marissa to get on with it.

"You shouldn't have. Really." Marissa shook her head at them. "When I said we should celebrate, I meant taking a few bottles of wine back to my house after work and starting in on our annual Christmas decorating."

"Pfft." Clara gave her an impatient look. "It's your five-year anniversary of owning this place. It deserves more than a regular Friday night in Christmas Grove."

Marissa stared at her two best friends and had to fight back tears. When she'd first arrived in Christmas Grove, she didn't know anyone. She'd been a twenty-nine-year-old with one failed marriage under her belt, who'd recently lost her only parent, her beloved father, and had been looking for a new start. She'd used her modest inheritance to put a down payment on the pub and to buy a small two-bedroom house. Besides opening the pub, her house had been the best decision she'd ever made because she'd lucked out in the neighbor department. Felicity had rented a room from Clara, her next-door neighbor, just days later, and the three of them had been besties ever since.

"Open. Open. Open," Felicity chanted as she handed Marissa one of the packages.

Marissa blinked back her tears and tore into the box. She held up a red apron that had the words *Did someone say Christmas brunch* printed above a fancy glass of egg nog. She snickered and immediately put the apron on. "Thank you. I love it."

"Good. But just so you know, that's a hint. I expect nog when we do the annual decorating," Felicity said with a wink.

"What else is new?" Marissa rolled her eyes playfully. Being a professional bartender meant she was always in charge of libations.

"Come on, open the rest before people start coming

in," Clara ordered, holding her phone up, ready to take pictures.

"Yes, bossy," Marissa teased and went to work opening the remaining gifts. They'd outdone themselves. By the time all the paper was ripped apart and the boxes opened, her haul consisted of a magical painting of the pub, complete with falling snow, and a T-shirt that had three cartoonish women standing together, holding hands. One was a blonde, one was brunette, and the other was a redhead, clearly depicting each of them. The redhead on the right had her hand raised with magic sparking from her palm, and the word *Charmed* was scrolled across the top. It was an homage to their favorite television show, *Charmed.*

She held the shirt up, admiring it, and then hugged it to her chest. "This is amazing. Where did you find it?"

Felicity made a show of buffing her nails. "I designed it and ordered it online."

"You're amazing." Marissa hugged her and then moved on to Clara. "No one could ask for better friends."

"We know," Clara said, her eyes sparkling. "Now finish up so we can start happy hour."

Chuckling, Marissa tore into the rest of her presents. The other gifts were a broom for above the door to keep the bad spirits out and a large bag of ornaments that were replicas of the spirits she kept behind the bar.

"You girls are too much," Marissa said, shaking her head.

"We're just the right amount," Felicity said just as the

door opened and Zach Frost strode in with a large Douglas fir tree.

"Special delivery," he said, grinning at the women. "Where do you want it?"

A couple walked in behind him and came up to the bar, picking up the order they'd called in. While she was ringing them up, the phone rang again. It stopped mid-ring, indicating that Jackson had gotten it.

Clara hurried over to Zach, directing where to put the tree that had to be at least eight feet tall.

When Marissa was done helping the couple, she walked over to Zach. "I didn't order a tree." Not that she hadn't wanted one, she'd just spent so many years pinching her pennies that it felt extravagant to purchase a live tree when her fake one was sitting in a storage closet.

"I did," Felicity said. "We live in Christmas Grove, Mar. Your establishment should have a live tree. That fake pine stuff you like to spray around just isn't the same."

Marissa frowned. "You never said anything before."

"Of course not. We knew you were doing your best. And honestly, if we could have afforded it, we'd have gotten you a live tree every other year. This year has been good to me, so I decided it was time."

Marissa squeezed her friend's hand and thanked Zach, the owner of Christmas Grove's Christmas tree farm, as he finished adjusting the tree stand.

"My pleasure, Marissa," he said, tipping his ball cap.

"Please stay and have a drink with us," Marissa said, waving to the bar.

"Wish I could, but things are hopping at the farm, and I have a few more deliveries to make," he said.

"Well, okay, but your next drink is on me," Marissa promised.

"It's a deal." He shook her hand and then waved goodbye to Felicity and Clara.

Marissa headed back to the bar and started cleaning up the wrapping paper.

"Wait!" Clara said. "You missed one." She held out a small box that had been hiding behind one of the bags.

"More?" Marissa shook her head at her friends. "You really went way overboard."

"That's what friends are for." Clara grinned.

Marissa opened the package and pulled out the loveliest glazed pottery mug she'd ever seen. It was red with a speckled white rim and had her custom logo on the front that said *Sleighed* with an outline of a sleigh that was loaded with bottles of spirits. "Oh my gosh. This is just... I love it."

"I knew you would," Clara said. "I ordered it from the new potter a few doors down. He nailed it, don't you think?"

"Yeah. He certainly did," she said, trying to force herself to sound grateful as she clutched the mug in both hands, suddenly wanting to throw the mug across the room. *Danny* had made the mug? She carefully placed the mug on the counter and went back to work cleaning up the space.

Just as she finished bagging the wrapping paper, the door swung open again, and in walked none other than

Danny Frost, the last person on the planet she ever wanted to see again.

She cleared her throat. "Danny, what are you doing here?"

The tall handsome man with dark hair and deep green eyes said, "I called in an order."

Jackson came out from the kitchen, holding a to-go bag. He smiled at Danny. "Good timing, man."

The pair bumped knuckles, and then Jackson rang up his order.

"We still on for that drink later?" Danny asked as he paid Jackson.

"Yep. Meet me here at nine-thirty after the kitchen closes." Jackson clapped him on the shoulder and headed back to the kitchen.

Danny glanced at Marissa. "Is that going to be okay with you?"

Marissa did everything in her power to keep her face neutral as she shrugged. "It's a free country."

"That it is." He nodded at Felicity and Clara and said, "Thanks, Marissa. I appreciate the hospitality." Then his eyes locked on the mug he'd made. He paused for a moment and then met Marissa's eyes. "I hope it's okay I took that commission."

Marissa cleared her throat and forced out, "Of course."

He nodded and left without another word.

"What was that all about?" Clara demanded.

"Nothing. What do you mean?" Marissa didn't meet her friend's eyes.

Clara picked up the mug. "Why would it matter if he took the commission?"

"It's a long story," Marissa said.

Felicity snorted. "Isn't it obvious? Marissa has history with the hot potter. Way to go, Mar. I wouldn't mind rolling around in the mud with that one. For a night at least."

Marissa jerked her head up, horrified at the thought of her best friend and Danny fooling around. "He's off limits," she heard herself say and then winced.

Clara's brows shot up as Felicity chuckled and said, "Yeah, there's a lot of history there." Then she pulled up a bar stool and said, "There's a story here. Spill."

Marissa sighed, glanced at the door, and then joined her friend. "It's a long story."

CHAPTER 2

$\mathcal{D}$anny Frost hung his head as he walked back to his pottery studio. Twelve months ago, when he'd spent the Christmas season in Christmas Grove with his grandmother, parents, and his cousins Atlas and Alison, the small Christmas town had seemed like the perfect place for a fresh start. Not only did he have the precious memories of his grandmother's last days before she passed, but he had cousins there. Atlas and his wife, Payton, now lived in town when he wasn't touring with his band. And Zach owned the Christmas tree farm that had been part of the fabric of Christmas Grove for generations.

What better place to finally open the pottery studio he'd been dreaming about for over a decade? After Christmas last year, he'd gone home to San Francisco, sold his apartment, and wound down his accounting business. Then after Atlas and Payton checked out the building that had been for sale on Main Street, they'd reported that it would be perfect for a pottery studio, so he'd purchased it sight unseen. By October, he'd moved and had begun to get his pottery shop ready for his grand opening in November. Never in all of that time had he realized that Marissa Cane, the love of his life and the woman he'd left after only six months of marriage, had relocated to Christmas Grove and opened her own business.

How that had happened, he wasn't quite sure. Marissa had been one hundred percent a city girl. He knew she'd had fond memories of passing through the town on her trips to Tahoe with her dad, but she'd never expressed interest in living anywhere but the city. Then again, it had been years since they'd last spoken. People changed. Circumstances changed. His certainly had.

Still, he couldn't help wondering if it was possible that Marissa had moved to Christmas Grove hoping to see him again. After all, she had known that his cousin Zach lived there.

No way.

Why would she think Danny would end up in Christmas Grove? Not to mention the fact that she'd walked into his pottery shop on the night of his grand opening and given him a piece of her mind. She hadn't been happy that he'd taken up residence in the magical town.

And really, could he blame her?

The way things ended with them... He'd still be angry, too.

He sat at the one table in his pottery studio that he kept clean of any clay and glazes and opened the takeout bag he'd gotten from her pub. So far, he'd done his best to steer clear of Marissa, but that day when he'd tried to call in an order at the pizzeria across the street, he'd learned that they were closed for a private party.

There were other places to get takeout, but he was in the mood for bar food. And he'd just decided that since it appeared that neither of them was going to close shop and move on, it was about time that they learned to live with each other. She didn't need to ever come into his pottery shop, but she owned the only bar with real pub food in the small mountain town. He couldn't stay away forever, could he?

No, he definitely couldn't. Not even if he tried.

He opened the takeout box and then devoured the best damned burger he'd had in months. After he finished off the fries, he cleaned up the area and then went back to his pottery wheel. He had a number of pieces to throw before it was time to meet Jackson.

DANNY'S SHOULDERS ACHED, and he was more than ready for that drink when he walked back into Sleighed. The moment he saw Marissa behind the bar, all of his minor aches and pains vanished. A smile tugged at his lips, but he instantly resumed a neutral expression when she scowled at him.

What had he expected? That she'd magically forgiven

him? There had been zero evidence of that when she'd walked into his studio last month and gave him a piece of her mind.

"Danny, good to see you, man," Jackson said, striding toward him with two mugs of beer. "I got you the lager, but if you'd prefer something else—"

"It's perfect," Danny said, taking one of the mugs. "Thanks."

"Sure," Jackson said and nodded toward a table in the corner on the other side of the stone fireplace. They'd met when Jackson had come into the studio asking about classes. He'd wanted a gift certificate for his mother, who'd said she always wanted to learn to play with clay. After they started talking, they'd learned they both had a passion for the outdoors, and they'd bonded over skiing and snowshoeing. And while Danny didn't have time to spend a day on the slopes, he had taken to early morning snowshoeing excursions with his new friend.

"How's business?" Jackson asked. "Busy for the holiday?"

"Very." Danny took a long sip of the beer and made an effort to relax his shoulders. "I never imagined I'd be turning over this much stock so soon. It's exhausting but a good problem to have." It was why Danny was working late to throw more mugs and pots. With the Christmas season upon them, both the residents and tourists of Christmas Grove had really embraced his wares.

"That's great, man." Jackson took a long pull of his beer. "At this rate, you'll need to hire help."

"Are you offering?" Danny asked, raising one eyebrow.

Jackson sputtered out a laugh. "In all my free time? Marissa keeps me pretty busy here."

"It was worth a shot." The truth was, he did need someone to man the shop so that he could replenish the shelves that were starting to look a little bare. If he didn't get someone in soon, his shelves would be empty. "If you know of anyone, send them my way."

Jackson nodded, looking thoughtful, but ultimately shook his head. "You know, I can't think of one person who might have some spare time. Most people start hiring seasonal workers before Halloween, and anyone who needed a job has already committed somewhere."

Danny sighed. He'd heard that from Payton already. How could he have known that he'd need help so soon? Still, being busy was a good problem to have, and he vowed to count his blessings.

"I'm going snowshoeing in the morning," Jackson said. "Are you in?"

It was their Saturday morning ritual and the one day a week that Danny never missed. He craved the fresh air and silence of the Sierras. If he had time during the week, he'd join Jackson more often, but that was becoming rarer and rarer the closer it got to Christmas. "I wouldn't miss it. Where are we headed this time?"

While Jackson talked about the trail he'd chosen, Danny heard a faint but distinct voice tell someone that it was time to go. He turned and scanned the bar, instantly locking his gaze on Marissa. She was standing with her balled fists pressed against her hips as she stared down a large man in jeans and a flannel shirt, her fiery energy radiating from her.

A sudden vision of the man grabbing Marissa by the hair and throwing her against the bar as the taser in her hand rolled to the floor flashed in his mind, and before he could spare another thought, he was on his feet and striding toward them.

"I'm not going until I get that drink," the red-faced man said with a sneer as he leaned over the bar. "You served everyone else."

Marissa straightened her shoulders and seemed to grow at least two inches taller as she stared the man down. "That isn't relevant to this situation, sir." Her voice was steady and filled with ice-cold determination. "By my calculations, you've had more than your fair share this evening. You won't be getting another drink here tonight."

Danny eyed the woman he'd been in love with since they were both fourteen years old and admired her conviction. She'd always been a fireball, but this version standing in front of him was impressive.

The man looked like he was ready to bite her head off as he balled his hand into a fist and then suddenly raised his arm in a threatening manner as he snarled, "You have no right to police my alcohol intake, you little—"

"That's enough!" Danny demanded, grabbing the man's arm and twisting it so that it was lodged against the man's back.

"Get off me!" the man growled as he bent forward, trying to buck Danny off him. Jackson appeared next to

Danny, and the two men quickly subdued the man and hauled him out the front door.

"Don't come back. Ever. Understand?" Jackson barked at the man.

Danny watched as the man flipped them off, jumped into a raised Ford Bronco, and then peeled off down the street, leaving black rubber marks on the road.

"He definitely shouldn't be driving," Danny said, frowning as he watched the Bronco speed away.

Jackson already had his phone to his ear. A second later, he said, "I need to report a drunk driver."

Danny patted his friend on the shoulder and reached for the door. Before he could grab the handle, it swung open and Marissa came barreling through, colliding right into him.

She stumbled and placed her hands on his chest to catch her fall as the door slammed closed behind her. "Oomph!"

Danny grabbed her arms, steadying her. "Are you all right?"

"Of course I'm all right," she said as she shook him off and then took a step back, crossing her arms over her chest. "Is he gone?"

"Yes," Jackson said, moving to stand next to Danny. "I called the sheriff to warn them he's not safe."

Her expression softened as she looked at Jackson. "Thank you for that." Then she glanced at Danny again before asking Jackson, "Can you give us a minute?"

"Sure, boss." Jackson nodded to Danny before disappearing back into the pub.

Once it was just the two of them, Marissa pressed her lips into a thin line before she said in a low, steady voice, "I didn't need you to rescue me. I had it under control." She held up the taser that had been in his vision. "I'm not the helpless female you think I am."

Danny nodded. "I know you're not helpless, but things were about to go south."

"Ha! About to? They were already south, Danny," she said, sounding exasperated. "I'm not sure who you think I am these days, but it's not the naive nineteen-year-old you wouldn't stick around and fight for sixteen years ago. How about you do me a favor and just stay out of my business now. All right? I can take care of myself."

"Marissa—" he started, but she held her hand up.

"I don't want to hear it. I'm sure you saw some vision, and instead of warning me so I could do something about it, you took matters into your own hands... again. Thanks, but no thanks." She turned on her heel and stomped back into the pub.

Danny ran a hand through his hair and blew out a long breath. Coming to Sleighed had been a mistake. Marissa definitely wasn't happy to see him. But there was no denying that he'd stopped that drunk from hurting her, and that was why he didn't regret a thing.

Jackson walked back out and stood with his hands in his jacket pockets. He rocked back on his heels and said, "So, do you want to tell me what's going on with you and Marissa?"

"There's nothing going on," Danny said, trying to ignore the pang of longing that always seemed to sneak up on him when he was talking about his ex. A light snow started to fall, making him even more melancholy. Marissa had always liked the snow. It was one of her favorite things. No wonder she'd moved to a place like Christmas Grove.

And maybe, if he was honest with himself, it might have been part of the reason why he had too.

"There's definitely something there, man. Anyone can see it a mile away," Jackson said.

Danny glanced at his friend and frowned. "There was at one time, but that's ancient history. Now we're just footnotes in each other's stories who just happened to run into each other again."

Jackson studied him. "History? I haven't known Marissa to date in all the years I've worked here. It must be really old history."

"Sixteen years," Danny said and then started to walk toward his Toyota 4Runner that was parked at the end of the block. After he took a few steps, he glanced over his shoulder and said, "See you at sunrise."

Jackson nodded once. "You bet."

As Danny got into his SUV, Jackson's words stuck in his mind. *I haven't known Marissa to date in all the years I've worked here.* And although he wasn't proud to admit it, that information made him happier than he had any right to be.

CHAPTER 3

"*irl,*" Felicity said, her tone full of sass as she strode into Marissa's house holding three pints of ice cream. "You have some explaining to do."

"Yes, you certainly do," Clara added, taking one of the ice cream containers from Felicity. "Earlier all you told us was that you had history with Danny the potter and you'd explain later. Well, it's time to pay up." She pointed at Marissa. "And we want all the gritty details. Not a washed down version because you don't want to talk about it."

Marissa sank into her oversized chair and curled up in the corner. Her sable-colored Havanese pup jumped up onto the ottoman and then snuggled in next to her, putting her head right under Marissa's hand, demanding to be petted.

Why did Marissa have friends again? All she really needed was her sweet pup, Pumpkin, and a roof over her head. Right? At least Pumpkin would never make her talk about Danny.

Felicity held out the pint of chocolate caramel swirl, and suddenly Marissa remembered why she loved her friends. They always brought her favorite ice cream when she needed it most.

"You're a goddess," Marissa said, tearing the top off.

Felicity just nodded as she held out a spoon.

Marissa took it and dove into the creamy goodness.

Once her two friends were seated on the couch across from her, they stared her down, waiting in silence.

Marissa knew they'd wait all night if they had to. After her third spoonful of the sinful treat, she sighed and said, "Danny Frost is my ex-husband."

"What?" Clara gasped, her eyes nearly bugging out.

"Your ex?" Felicity asked, looking thoughtful. "So your disdain for marriage comes from personal experience." It was a statement, not a question.

"It does," Marissa agreed, knowing they weren't going to let her just drop it. But still she stalled. It had been years since she'd talked about Danny to anyone. If she had her way, she wouldn't say a word about him now either.

"How long ago did you get divorced? It must have been at least five years ago," Clara speculated as she dug a spoonful of coffee ice cream out of her container.

"Sixteen." Marissa petted Pumpkin, not looking at her friends.

"Sixteen!" they both exclaimed at the same time.

Felicity looked horrified as she quickly did the math. "You got divorced at nineteen? How old were you when you got married? Did your parents sell you off as a child bride or something?"

Marissa gave her an exasperated look. "No. My parents didn't sell me into marriage. Come on. Danny and I were best friends, and then we dated all through high school. We made it through one year of college before we decided we were tired of waiting and eloped in Vegas. I was a few weeks shy of turning nineteen, while he'd been nineteen for a whole month and a half."

"Oh, Marissa," Clara said, clutching her chest with her right hand. "You were together for five years before you got married? What made it all fall apart?"

"They were dumb teenagers," Felicity piped in. "What do you think happened?" She turned to Marissa. "Did he cheat? Do drugs? Steal your money? My grandmother used to say that men don't actually come into their brains until they're at least thirty. And you know, I'd say that the young men I know prove her right more often than not."

Clara rolled her eyes. "You know I hate it when you say that. First of all, it's not true. Second, if it were true, that would just be giving young men an excuse to be shitty."

"It's not an excuse. It just is," Felicity shot back. "Prove me wrong. Name me one man under thirty who hasn't completely effed something up because they were thinking with something other than their brains."

As Clara started naming off men she knew from town, Marissa sat back, watching her friends spar. She was in no hurry to continue her story. It was ancient history now anyway. All she had to do was figure out how she could keep her distance from Danny, and everything would be fine. Right?

That was all well and good, but it wasn't like she could ban him from Sleighed. Technically, she guessed she could. She did run a private business, after all, but she would never be so cruel as to ban the man from her pub just because he shattered her heart sixteen years ago. She was over him. What did it matter if he came in for takeout or to have drinks with Jackson? As long as he stayed out of her business, they'd be just fine.

"Earth to Marissa. Are you still with us?" Felicity called, waving her hands to get her attention.

Marissa blinked and shook her head slightly, clearing her thoughts. "What is it? What'd I miss?"

"Everything apparently." Felicity jerked a thumb at the back door. "You didn't even hear Pumpkin barking to go out."

Marissa looked down at her chair and frowned when she saw Pumpkin was gone. She hadn't even noticed her dog getting up. How out of it was she? Marissa hopped up out of the chair and opened the back door for her pooch while she grabbed a thick sweatshirt that hung on a hook on the wall. Even though the area was fenced, Marissa never let her little twelve-pound baby out by herself. There was too much wildlife that preyed on small animals.

When Pumpkin had sniffed every inch of the yard and finally relieved herself in her preferred spot, she came running full speed back to Marissa, her tongue hanging out and her eyes sparkling with mischief.

"You goof." Marissa let Pumpkin in and went back to her friends, who were waiting for her in the living room.

"We put the ice cream away," Clara said. "That cake earlier and now ice cream was probably a little much."

Marissa raised one eyebrow. "There's always room for ice cream."

Felicity let out a bark of laughter. "Well, it's in the freezer. Help yourself."

"Nah. I'll save it for tomorrow." Marissa got comfortable in her seat again with Pumpkin and wished she'd thought to make herself a cup of decaf.

"All right. What happened? You married your high school sweetheart, and then he bolted. Why?" Clara asked, leaning forward with her hands clasped in her lap.

"I'd bet a month's salary that he met someone else," Felicity said with a frown. Then under her breath, she added, "Men are so predictable."

"You'd lose that bet." Marissa picked up the comb on her side table and started combing Pumpkin's hair just to have something else to focus on. "It wasn't someone else. At least not the way you're thinking."

"What does that mean?" Clara asked.

"That's cryptic." Felicity grabbed a bottle of wine that had appeared while Marissa had been taking Pumpkin out and poured a generous amount into a wine glass before handing it to Marissa. "Some liquid courage."

"Thank you." Marissa gave her a grateful smile and downed almost half the contents of the glass before she came up for air. "Okay, so we got married. My dad wasn't thrilled, but he'd known Danny for years and loved him too. So even though we were young, he accepted it and helped us get our own studio apartment."

"Your dad always sounds like the dad everyone wishes they had," Felicity said, sounding wistful. "If only my mother had better taste in men."

Clara and Marissa both chuckled. Felicity's parents had gotten divorced when she was fifteen because her dad had fallen in love with the neighbor's wife. When both marriages imploded, he'd left Felicity's mom and moved in next door. Despite that, Felicity still rarely saw him, and he'd basically checked out of her life the moment he'd left her mom.

"He *was* that kind of dad," Marissa said, a sad smile tugging at her lips. Her dad had been her best friend and the one person in the world she'd always counted on. At one time, she'd thought she'd always have Danny, too, but he'd ruined that for her. "I miss him every day."

Clara reached out and squeezed Marissa's hand but didn't say anything. They all knew that Marissa's grief still came in waves. Her dad had been her person.

"Anyway," Marissa said, suddenly determined to finish her story. The longer she dragged it out, the longer her stomach would be in knots. "One day Danny told me he had a terrible vision that involved both of us and that he had to leave."

"Vision? Is he a seer or something?" Clara asked.

"Yes. He'd get flashes of things that were about to happen. If the vision indicated someone was going to get hurt, he'd step in to help. If it was a good vision, he'd often stop and wait so I could witness it, too. Like the time we witnessed the sweetest proposal or when a dog and his owner were reunited.

"Danny just came into our room, his face almost gray as he told me that he loved me but he had to leave. That he had no other choice. And then with tears in his eyes, he packed his stuff and left. It was the last time I saw him."

"He didn't even tell you what his vision was about?" Clara was clutching her chest as if the story had pained her.

"No. He refused. Six months later, the divorce paperwork showed up. That night I ate an entire cheesecake and then, feeling like I was going to throw up, I signed the papers."

"Well, sure," Felicity chimed in. "An entire cheesecake will do that to a person."

"Felicity!" Clara admonished. "Clearly the cheesecake was just one of the issues. The love of her life walked out on her and then just sent divorce papers. That's really cold."

"It sounds like he left to protect her," Felicity said, eyeing Marissa. "That's the short version, right?"

"Yeah," Marissa agreed. "But he didn't tell me about the vision or give me any chance to change the future. For all I know, his vision came true anyway and I survived just fine."

"You really think that?" Felicity asked.

"No, but it could have happened." Marissa knew enough about his visions to know that, when he stepped in, he usually did change the outcome. Her most burning question was, why hadn't he stayed to fight for her?

Instead he'd just left, leaving her so devastated that she still carried the wound with her.

"What I want to know is why did he have to move to *my* town?" Marissa complained. "After all this time, why did he end up here?"

Clara and Felicity shared a knowing glance.

Marissa narrowed her eyes at them. "What?"

Finally Clara cleared her throat. "He does have family here. Aren't Zach and Atlas his cousins?"

"Yes, but he was never close to them! I don't know why he'd suddenly move here out of nowhere. It just seems suspect." Marissa knew she sounded petulant, but Danny's presence in the town she'd grown to love so much was really messing with her.

"Mar, don't take this the wrong way, but I think the same question could be asked of you," Clara continued. "I mean, you did move to a town where the Frosts have deep roots. If you really never wanted to see him again, why would you do that?"

"You're saying you think I moved here on the off chance that Danny might show up here? That's crazy." Marissa downed the rest of her wine. "If I wanted to stalk him, don't you think I'd have done that in San Francisco where he actually lived? Hanging out at his local coffee shop every morning would have been a lot more productive than this apparently elaborate long game."

Clara chuckled softly. "I'm not saying you wanted to actively stalk the man, but maybe it's possible that deep down you had an unconscious desire to be somewhere connected to him."

Marissa opened her mouth to protest the absurd theory, but Clara put her hand up, stopping her. "I might be way off," Clara continued. "I'm just saying things happen that none of us can explain. Sometimes the universe has plans that we don't understand right away. Maybe this reuniting will give you both a chance for closure and healing."

"I don't need closure," Marissa muttered. "That happened the day I signed the divorce papers."

Clara blew out a breath. "Sure. But clearly there's still a lot of anger where he's concerned. This could be your chance to put that behind you."

Marissa averted her gaze, knowing her friend was right. She did have a lot of anger issues when it came to Danny. She'd thought she was past it all, but seeing him thriving at his pottery studio and acting as if she didn't affect him at all was driving her crazy. If he was even just a little bit remorseful about leaving her all those years ago, then maybe she wouldn't feel so awful about it. But so far, the man hadn't apologized, and instead he acted as if them being in the same town wasn't bothering him at all. After how close they'd been, she just didn't understand it.

"Why did you move to Christmas Grove?" Felicity asked. "Other than wanting to open the pub, I don't think you've ever said."

"When we'd go up to Tahoe when I was a kid, my dad always stopped here on the way up and on the way home. We'd get breakfast at Candy Canes. I'd have the chocolate chip pancakes, and he'd have the French toast with extra bacon. And on the way back we'd stop again for dinner.

All I cared about was the hot chocolate with a mountain of whipped cream, but Dad loved the old-time feel of that diner." Marissa smiled. "I have a lot of happy memories here with my dad. I couldn't stay in his house. Not where he'd spent his last days. It was just too sad. What better way to honor him than to get my chocolate chip pancakes and hot chocolate every Sunday? It just makes me feel like he's smiling down on me."

Clara wiped the tears from her eyes. "That's why you always want to go there and always get the same thing."

"I just thought she had the taste buds of a ten-year-old," Felicity teased. "Either that or you were a trash panda in another life."

Marissa snickered. "Maybe I was. The only thing I know for sure is that those pancakes are just as good now as they were then, and as long as Candy Canes is open for business, I'll be there every Sunday morning."

"That's so sweet." Clara hopped up off the couch, went over to Marissa, and hugged her from behind. "I guess you really did move here with your dad in mind. It's just unfortunate for you that Danny had family ties here."

"Yeah," Marissa said softly, staring at the roaring fireplace. The thing was, deep down, she'd always known that at least a tiny part of the reason she chose Christmas Grove was because she felt a little bit closer to Danny there. But she'd never admit it. Not to Clara and Felicity, and certainly not to anyone else. She gathered Pumpkin in her arms and rose from her chair. "Enough of memory lane. Who's ready to start helping me decorate?"

"Now?" Felicity asked at the same time Clara rubbed her hands together and said, "Me!"

"Ugh." Felicity rolled her eyes. "Both of you are entirely too cheerful."

"It's why you love us. We keep you from being too grumpy," Marissa said and slipped her arm through Felicity's. "Now come on. We need your help getting the tree down out of the closet."

"You only keep me around for my height and extra-long reach," she complained.

"We also keep you because you always bring the wine," Marissa said, leaning in and nudging her playfully.

"I wouldn't be me without a stocked wine fridge," she said with a wink and then added, "Don't you think it's way too late to be doing this now? Can't we do it Sunday after we go to Candy Canes?"

Marissa glanced at the clock on the wall and winced when she saw it was almost midnight. While she knew she probably wouldn't get a wink of sleep after talking about Danny, it was pretty late for their decorating party. "Fine. Let's just get the tree down, and we can do the actual decorating Sunday." She smiled at Felicity. "Complete with nog."

Felicity grinned. "Deal."

CHAPTER 4

*D*anny walked into his apartment and dropped his keys in the bowl on the table next to the door. The scent of hay mixed with wood shavings and a hint of leather had become all too familiar since he'd moved into the one-bedroom place above the Jolly's barn.

When he'd moved to Christmas Grove, there hadn't been much to choose from in the rental department. There'd been a house with a leaky roof and what looked suspiciously like mold growing on the ceiling of the bathroom, a mobile home with windows that whistled anytime the wind blew, and a cabin that didn't have running water. None of which had been suitable for habitation. Although he had money for a down payment on a house, he really wanted to buy land and build a custom home. With no rental readily available, he started to explore buying land with the plan to get a fifth wheel as temporary housing until he was ready to break ground on his forever home.

While he was looking at the lot next door, Frederick Jolly, the owner of the Make it Jolly Ranch, had stopped by to say hello. While they were talking, Frederick had mentioned the barn apartment, and Danny had rented it that day. He'd purchased the land next door, too, only now he didn't have to live in a fifth wheel during the winter.

"Meow."

Danny looked down at the sweet black and white cat that was intertwining her body between his ankles and rubbing her head on his shin. He quickly scooped Bells up and gave her some scritches on her head. "Hey, you. Miss me?"

She closed her eyes as she leaned into his chest and started to purr.

He kissed her head and made his way into the kitchen. After grabbing a bottle of water, he retreated to the bedroom, placed Bells next to his pillow, and got ready for bed. Fifteen minutes later, he was under the covers with Bells snuggling his side.

The kitty was just over a year old and had been the one who'd been there through losing his grandmother, moving to a new town, and abruptly changing careers. It had been a lot, but Bells had been the one constant who was always there, ready to show him unconditional love any time he needed it.

And tonight, he needed it.

All the fear he'd lived with while he was married to Marissa had started to come crashing back as soon as he'd processed the fact that she'd almost been attacked. Toward the end of their relationship, he'd been on edge every single day, waiting for the worst to happen.

His shoulders and jaw ached with tension as he stared at the ceiling, telling himself that she ran a bar. An altercation could have happened at any time. Of course she'd run into belligerent drinkers every now and then. And by the looks of things, she'd done that plenty of times in the past. She hadn't needed him then.

But she had needed him tonight. At least that's what his vision had told him. It made him want to stay glued to her side to make sure she was safe.

Danny grunted his irritation at himself.

Marissa wasn't helpless, and it wasn't his job to watch over her. Those days were long gone. And she clearly didn't want his help. That didn't mean he'd stand by and do nothing if he had another vision though. How could he?

Sighing, Danny checked to make sure his alarm was set, turned out the light, and curled up on his side next to his cat, waiting for sleep to take him.

The moment he fell under, the dreaming started.

The sun shone down on the pristine white snow, warming Danny's skin as he sat in his porch swing, sipping his morning coffee. The peacefulness of the moment had settled in his bones, and if there was one word to describe him, it was content. His farmhouse was finally finished, and there was nothing he liked more than starting his morning at sunrise on his porch as he stared out at the mountains.

The door swung open, and a small sable-colored dog ran out of the house and straight for him. The sweet thing jumped up on his leg, excitedly asking for attention.

"You're awfully perky this morning," he said to the dog as he lifted her up to sit in his lap. She immediately bathed his face in kisses before settling down in his lap as he ran his hand over her soft, velvety fur.

"I see you two started your day without me," Marissa said, smiling down at them as she joined them on the porch. She had the mug he'd made for her that had her logo on the front in her hand, and it made his heart full.

"Come here," he said, patting the space next to him.

Without hesitation, she sat on the porch swing and curled in next to him. "This is my favorite place in the world."

"Mine too when you're here." He wrapped his arm around her, pulled her in closer, and gave her a gentle, lingering kiss.

She let out a contented sigh, pressed her head to his chest just over his heart and said, "Merry Christmas, Mr. Garland."

He stared down at her, and suddenly he knew now was the time. He pulled the small velvet box out of his pocket and placed it in her hand.

She jerked her head up, staring at him wide-eyed. "Is this what I think it is?"

His lips twitched into a tiny smile. "Maybe. Why don't you open it?"

She sat fully upright, and with trembling hands, she lifted the lid. Tears sprang into her violet eyes, and she blinked rapidly as the diamond sparkled in the light.

Danny slid out from underneath the pup and kneeled on the ground in front of her. After taking the ring out of the box, he took her left hand in his and felt his eyes sting with his own *tears as he held the ring up and said, "You're the love of my life. I can't imagine living this life another day without you and Pumpkin. Would you do me the honor of being my wife and letting me love you forever?"*

A crash sent him bolt upright, his heart thundering in his chest. He blinked, looking around at the darkness. Taking in the bedroom of his apartment, he felt a sinking disappointment all the way to his toes. He wasn't living in the new farmhouse that had felt so real in his dream.

There was no sweet dog.

And no Marissa.

He flipped the light on and squinted as his eyes adjusted. Bells was standing in the middle of the floor, licking her paw, seemingly oblivious to the broken lamp beside her.

Danny gritted his teeth as he got out of bed. The cold wood floor made him shiver as he quickly cleaned up the mess. "I've seen you navigate the dresser before," he said, admonishing his cat. "Even in the dark you seem to be able to get around fine. Do you really think this was necessary?"

The cat ignored him.

But as soon as he finished his chore, she pressed her warm body to his leg and looked up at him with adoring eyes.

"You have zero remorse," he said, scooping her up again. "Come on, little one. Let's get back in bed. This time though, try to get some sleep instead of terrorizing my things, okay?"

She rubbed her head on his chest and purred.

Once he was back under the covers, he placed her on his chest, needing the weight of the small creature for comfort.

It had been years since he'd dreamed of Marissa. And even then, his dreams had never felt so *real*. He could even still smell her honey scent as if she'd just been right next to him. He'd almost be willing to believe that it had been a vision, but she'd called him Mr. Garland. Which was weird. His last name was Frost. Why had his subconscious come up with that? Besides, his visions hadn't ever come to him as a dream before anyway.

No, this was just him missing her. Leaving her had left a hole in both his soul and his heart. Over the years, he'd learned to live with it, but now that they were in the same town and he could no longer pretend he'd never see her again, all of his emotions were coming to the surface.

He missed her.

And he still loved her.

That much was clear. But what could he do about it now? She hated him. And even if she didn't, what if it became clear that having him in her life would still put her in danger? He couldn't put either of them through that again. No matter how much he wanted her.

He let out a long-suffering sigh and closed his eyes, willing himself to fall into an unconscious oblivion. But it was a long time before he fell back asleep, and when he did, it was fitful. Finally, just before five, he got up, showered, and went to make the world's largest cup of coffee.

Once he had caffeine in his system, he fed Bells and

then got dressed, going through the motions as if he were in a fog. The dream the night before had felt so real. More real than anything he'd experienced in a long time. And the fact that it wasn't had left him despondent. He could only hope that some fresh air and physical exertion would pull him out of his gloomy mood.

When he stepped outside, he welcomed the bitter chill, preferring to feel something other than the disappointment that had stayed with him after he'd woken from his dream. When he got into his 4Runner, he drove to the trail to meet Jackson as if he were on autopilot.

"Morning!" Jackson called, sounding more chipper than anyone had a right to at sunrise on a cold winter morning. He tugged his gloves on and grinned at Danny. "I hope you had a good night's rest, 'cause I'm in the mood to put in some miles."

Danny grunted his reply.

"Uh-oh. Sounds like a bit of a rough night," Jackson said.

"Sort of." Danny pulled his snowshoes out of the 4Runner and went to work on snapping them to his boots.

"Want to talk about it?" Jackson asked as they moved toward the trail.

"Not really." Jackson worked for Marissa. He couldn't exactly tell him that he was still hung up on his ex, whom he hadn't seen or spoken to in the last sixteen years.

"Understandable, but if you change your mind, I'm a good listener." He clapped a hand on Danny's shoulder.

"Thanks, man."

Jackson nodded. They were silent for a few minutes before Jackson said, "Did I tell you that I used to be the regional vice president of Snow Valley Sports?"

Danny glanced over at the man who looked more like someone who'd spent his youth backpacking for months at a time instead of wearing a suit and answering to corporate overlords. "Seriously?"

His friend chuckled softly but then quickly sobered. "Yep. My dad was the CEO of a big financial institution. Growing up, I was very into sports. I ended up skiing competitively and almost made the Olympic team when I was a sophomore in college. Then a knee injury took me out, and that was the end of that. I lost my scholarship and my dreams all in one blow."

"Damn. That's rough," Danny said. "I'm sorry, man. But you must have finished school if you ended up a VP."

"Yeah, I did. But only after my father stipulated that I change my major to business." He made a face indicating he was not thrilled with that development. "See, I was a sports and recreational management major. I figured once my ski career was over, I'd go run a ski resort or backpacking company. Something where I could spend my days outdoors. But my father absolutely refused to pay for college unless I switched to straight business. So that's what I did. And the next thing I knew, I graduated and was on the corporate ladder."

Danny followed Jackson around a bend in the trail and was amazed when a pristine lake appeared, set against the backdrop of the mountains. "This is something else."

"Isn't it?" Jackson stopped to stare out at the glassy

water. "It's the type of place where you can just feel the magic."

There was wonder in the air. It was what Danny had felt the moment they'd appeared around the bend. Possibility. Joy. And hope. He slowly filled his lungs with the cold air, letting the beauty of the spot fill him.

"It's settles you, doesn't it?" Jackson asked.

"Yes." Ever since the day Marissa had walked into his shop, he'd been a little bit on edge. Not quite right. Maybe even second guessing his decision to move to Christmas Grove.

"I knew at a young age that this was what I wanted to spend my life experiencing, but I let outside forces tell me what I should do." Jackson stared at the lake as he spoke. "Corporate life was all consuming. A way to always acquire *more*. More power. More money. More things. The one thing it didn't give me was what I needed most."

"Happiness?" Danny guessed. He'd left his own unfulfilling job, after all. He was well acquainted with what it felt like to make a living doing something he didn't enjoy.

"Family." Jackson turned and looked at Danny. "It was just me and my father. My mom left when I was too young to remember. And when my father died from a heart attack at fifty-two, I looked around at my life and didn't like what I saw. My father killed himself working, and he worked so much that he didn't have any significant relationships. It was a wakeup call."

"So you quit your VP job and moved to Christmas Grove?" Danny asked, fascinated to learn more about the man who always seemed as if he were just part of the fabric of Christmas Grove.

"Sort of. I actually quit and followed a girl. She's the one who taught me to cook." He winked. "That didn't work out, but I did fall in love with this town. And now I have family. There are a lot of people who came to Christmas Grove looking for the same thing, and we share a bond. Marissa is one of them."

Danny stiffened, suddenly on edge. "Do you have a thing for Marissa?" He'd said he hadn't known Marissa to date anyone in the five years he'd known her. Was he hoping to be the one?

The other man laughed. "No, man. I'm just saying that I consider her family. That's all."

"Okay. Why do I get the feeling you're trying to tell me something?"

Jackson's lips quirked into a faint smile. "Maybe I am." He waved a hand at the magical view. "This view and this town, it's healing. It soothes the soul. But what's really important is family. Find yours, and everything else will fall into place."

Frowning, Danny watched as Jackson turned and started back on the trail.

When Danny didn't follow, Jackson turned and called, "Are you coming?"

"Yeah," he said with a sigh and hurried to catch up. When he got to Jackson's side he asked, "Are you an empath?"

Jackson paused and looked at him. "Was I that obvious?"

"Yes."

Silence fell between them, and Danny desperately wanted to ask how Marissa really felt about him moving to Christmas Grove, but he kept the thought to himself. There was no way Jackson would tell him anyway. It would be a breach of privacy. Eventually he said, "I'm a seer."

That stopped Jackson in his tracks. "Really? How does that work exactly?"

"I get visions of events that are about to happen, and then I can step in and change them... or not." Danny frowned. "Usually, anyway."

"Wow. That sounds like quite a burden." Jackson seemed genuinely concerned.

"It can be," Danny admitted.

Without Danny saying more, Jackson stared at him with clarity in his eyes and asked, "If you could get rid of the visions, would you?"

Danny hesitated a moment and then shook his head. If he helped even one person, it was worth it.

"I thought that was the case," Jackson said. "It's definitely a gift *and* a curse. I can sense that it weighs on your soul."

That was an understatement. His gift had taken the only person he'd ever loved from him.

"You're resentful, too." Jackson studied him, looking troubled. "My advice?"

Danny nodded, because after his dream last night, he was either going to scream or break something.

"Don't sacrifice yourself or your loved ones to your gift. Everyone loses then."

It was good advice, but it came sixteen years too late.

"Come on. It's getting late," Jackson said as he continued on with the walk. "Let's get moving so you can get to work."

Danny nodded and followed his friend, but for the next hour, all he could think about was what would have happened sixteen years ago if he hadn't let his visions rule his decisions.

CHAPTER 5

"It's time for Santa's little helper to get her shopping on," Marissa said as she walked into Clara's glass studio and gallery. Since Marissa didn't have to be into work until late afternoon, she'd spent her day baking, finishing up her Christmas cards, and was now tackling her holiday gift list. She'd been Santa's most productive elf that day and was feeling really good about herself.

Clara looked up from the desk, her red face pinched with irritation. Her dark hair was pulled up into a haphazard bun, and she was wearing a yellow leather apron that had burn marks on it.

"What happened to you?" Marissa asked, hurrying over to the counter and scanning Clara's body, looking for any signs that she'd gotten into a fight with her blow pipe. Other than a few leather burns, she seemed fine.

"My kiln is on the fritz. Can you believe it? It's three

weeks before Christmas, and my annealing kiln has given up the ghost. I'll never get a new one in here before the holiday. All those orders I have waiting for me are going to disappear into thin air. Not to mention my private clients are going to be very disappointed." She groaned and pressed her hand to her forehead. "Atlas was going to make Payton something special for Christmas. Can you believe that I had to tell *the rock star* Atlas Mazer that he's going to have to go down to Fire on the River if he wants to follow through on that idea? Now he'll likely take lessons there instead of here, and my delusions of becoming besties with him are shot. He'll tell all of his fans where he made his gift, and they'll be ordering from there instead of from me. And just when I was starting to think I might be able to trade in my beater car for something that has a working heater."

Marissa raised her eyebrows and blinked at her. "Whoa. Slow down, Clara. You're spiraling. I'm sure we can figure this out. Can't you order a kiln with overnight shipping?"

"It's not just shipping," Clara said with a deep sigh. "Kilns are generally made to order. Especially the one I have. Even if they could do a rush order, it's not going to get here in time."

"We should make some calls," Marissa said. "Find out if there's one anywhere nearby that we can pick up." She slipped behind the counter and tapped Clara's computer to wake up the screen, and then she started googling.

The bell on the door chimed, but Marissa was too busy

searching for local suppliers to pay any attention. Then she heard his voice.

"Atlas said you're having a kiln problem."

Marissa jerked her head up to find Danny standing in the store, wearing jeans and a sweatshirt. Both were smudged with clay, making it clear he'd just come from his studio.

Clara nodded glumly. "It shorted out today. I can't get it to do anything. Three weeks before Christmas, and I'm out of production."

"Do you mind if I take a look at it?" Danny asked. "I built two of mine. I might be able to fix it or rig something that will work until you can get it repaired."

"Repaired?" Clara asked as if the notion hadn't even occurred to her. "I never even considered that since it would take even longer for a repair than to order a new one. Besides, some of the bricks are chipped, and now that the wiring is bad, I figured I'd better just replace it."

"You built kilns?" Marissa asked, shocked. He hadn't exactly been the handiest guy when they were kids. Though he did make pottery for a living now, so clearly they'd both changed a lot.

"Yeah. It's faster and, if you can get the materials, cheaper, too." He turned his attention to Clara. "Mind if I take a look at it?"

"Oh, gosh. Not at all," Clara gushed as she started to walk toward the door that led to her hot shop. "If you can fix it, I'll cook for you for a month. Mow your lawn. Wash your car. You name it; I'll do it."

He chuckled. "That won't be necessary. I'm just happy to help."

Marissa hurried after them, and as Danny started to poke around the kiln, she asked, "Why did Atlas call you to tell you Clara's kiln was broken?"

"He didn't call to tell me that," Danny said, using the flashlight on his smart phone to get a better look at the wiring. "He called for something else and happened to mention it."

"And you just came running?" Her tone was more accusatory than she'd intended, but she really didn't understand why her ex was suddenly all up in Clara's business.

"Something like that." He glanced at Clara. "Do you have a screwdriver?"

"Sure." She grabbed a small toolkit and handed it to him.

As Danny began taking the kiln apart, Clara walked over to Marissa and bumped her shoulder. "Stop antagonizing the only person who might be able to help me."

"I was going to help!" Marissa frowned at her friend. "Remember me offering to call all the suppliers within driving distance?"

"Sure, I remember, but there are only like two in the state, so your chances were pretty slim."

"At least I was going to try," Marissa muttered.

"And I truly appreciate that." Clara grabbed her arm and leaned in for a hug. "But if Danny can get me back up and running, he'll be my own personal hero."

"Aha!" Danny called out. "I've found the issue."

"What?" Clara ran over to him. "Can it be fixed?"

"Sure. It's just a fuse in the controller. Once it's changed, you should be back up and running." He held up the offending part. "Let me run back to my studio to see if I have one. If not, you can get one overnighted."

"Danny, I think the sugar plum fairies sent me my own Christmas miracle. Thank you!" Clara threw herself at him, hugging him with everything she had.

He chuckled awkwardly and met Marissa's gaze. He had a bewildered look, and Marissa just shrugged. That was Clara. She never held back affection for those she cared about.

It was strange watching her best friend form a friendship with Danny. At one time, she'd known him better than she knew herself, and when he bolted from their life together, a hole had formed in her heart. And as far as she could tell, it still hadn't healed.

It was a Danny-shaped hole, and watching him hug her best friend was really messing with her. She turned abruptly and walked back into the gallery. She had come in that afternoon specifically to purchase gifts for her staff. Every year, she got each of them an ornament from Clara's, and then she went and got fresh apple pies from Felicity's family farm, Apples and Spice and Everything Nice. After five years, it was a tradition now.

She walked over to the tree that was decorated with glass ball ornaments and inspected each one until she found three, all different, but each iridized with silver, blue, and purple swirls.

Marissa was on her way to the register when the most gorgeous snow globe caught her eye. Inside there was a scene of downtown Christmas Grove, and without even shaking it, the snow was continuously falling, blanketing the brick sidewalk. The base was a gorgeous Christmas red, complete with a ribbon of white glass that had been manipulated into a bow. Very carefully, she picked up the globe. It immediately started to play "Christmas Time is Here" by Vince Guaraldi. A very vivid memory of her and Danny decorating their first and last Christmas tree flashed in her mind. The song had come on, and instead of finishing putting up the garland, Danny had taken her in his arms, and they'd swayed to the music in the pale glow of the Christmas tree lights.

Tears stung her eyes as memories washed over her. She'd been at her happiest that year. Danny had surprised her with a weekend trip to Tahoe even though they were broke and barely had enough for the gas to get there and back. The owner of the coffee shop he worked at had a condo up there and had scheduled a delivery for new appliances. When he had a scheduling conflict and couldn't make it up there, he'd offered the cabin to Danny if he'd just be there when the appliances were changed out. For an hour of their time, they'd had a wonderful three-day weekend in the snow.

And Danny had somehow budgeted enough so that they could stop at Candy Canes in Christmas Grove, both on the way up and the way back. That weekend was full of her fondest memories.

She blinked back the tears and took the snow globe up

to the counter. It looked like this year, she was getting a present from Clara's shop, too.

"Marissa? Are you all right?" Danny asked from right behind her, making her jump. She'd been so busy staring at her snow globe that she hadn't even heard them come back into the gallery.

She spun, praying that her eyes weren't red from her tears. "Yeah. Just getting my shopping done." She averted her gaze, suddenly feeling uncomfortable. He always used to be able to see right through her.

He glanced at the counter where her wares were waiting and then back at her. "Great choice. I might need to get some of those for my tree."

"You have a tree?" As soon as she heard the words come out of her mouth, she wanted to claw them back. Of course he had a tree. His cousin owned the local Christmas tree farm. It would be criminal if he was a bah humbug and never bothered to make his house festive.

"Actually, no, not yet. I'm heading up to Zach's tomorrow to see if I can find one that will fit into my apartment." He held up a part in his hand. "Right now, I need to see if I have one of these so Clara doesn't miss any holiday business." He headed for the door.

Marissa called after him. "It's really nice of you to help her out. I appreciate it, and I know she does too."

He glanced back at her. "Thanks, but I'm just being a good neighbor." Danny stepped back and waved as he retreated through the front door.

Clara appeared from the hot shop, a smile lighting her face. "It looks like Danny Frost might save Christmas after all." Her gaze landed on the items on the counter, and her expression softened. "I wondered if that globe was going to catch your eye."

"You should have just sent me an invoice." Marissa chuckled softly. "It's just so lovely, Clara. Really, you've outdone yourself."

Clara flushed with pleasure as she stepped behind the counter to ring up Marissa's purchases. After wrapping everything up, she announced a total that was less than half of the retail price.

"That total isn't right," Marissa said, eyeing her friend. "Redo it."

"It's right," she insisted, holding the paper bag out to Marissa.

"It's not," Marissa insisted. "I'm not going to let you shortchange yourself just because we're friends."

Clara raised one eyebrow. "Keep arguing and the total is going to go down."

"Seriously? I'm just going to find a way to pay you back later," Marissa said. "Two can play this game, you know."

"Yep. I can't even remember the last time I paid for a drink at Sleighed, so it seems we're already even." Clara put her finger over the point-of-sale system. "Now, are you going to pay, or am I going to discount this further?"

"You're impossible." Marissa shook her head at her and tapped her credit card on the screen.

The door swung open again, and Danny walked in, holding a small part in his hand. "I found one! Give me ten minutes and you'll be good to go."

Clara let out a squeal and ran over to him. "You are my new favorite person!"

He grinned and the two of them disappeared into the hot shop again.

With her shopping bag in hand, Marissa followed and stood near the door as she listened to them talk about the holiday art and craft shows that were coming up.

"I'm sure you know about the one at the Christmas tree farm," Clara said. "But what about the one during the tree lighting? Did you snag a table?"

"No. I wish I could have, but I wasn't sure I'd have enough product. To be honest, I'm not even sure I'll have enough to keep my shelves stocked anyway," he said. "Business has been better than expected, and I just don't have enough time between manning the shop and trying to create new work."

"Well, that's not the worst problem to have," Clara said. "You need to hire some help."

He chuckled. "I'd love to, but I can't seem to find anyone with time. So for now, I'm burning the midnight oil." Danny had gotten the part installed and was busy replacing the metal plate that housed the electronics. "Though I really would have liked to be part of that art show. If for nothing else than to introduce myself to the residents who haven't had a chance to come into the shop."

Clara brightened. "You can share my table."

Marissa stared at her friend, open mouthed. She did remember that Danny was her ex, right? Why was she acting like he was her new best friend? Or worse, someone she was interested in. Marissa shook her head. There was no way Clara was contemplating dating him. She didn't have a callous bone in her body. And Marissa knew that both of her friends would walk through traffic for her. She needed to get out of there before her imagination got any more active.

"I'm gonna take off," Marissa called.

They both turned to look at her, and it was obvious to Marissa that neither of them had even known she was standing there.

"Let me walk you out," Clara said.

"That's not necessary. I'm headed over to Apples and Spice for pies. Do you need anything?"

"I'm good," Clara said, glancing between her and Danny. "Now that my knight in shining armor has shown up."

Marissa rolled her eyes, and instead of saying something she'd regret, she just waved and left.

When she got outside, she leaned against the building, trying to regain control of her emotions. Watching Danny acting like the boy she'd known all those years ago had made her feel as if she'd been gut punched. And it wasn't because she seriously thought her friend was interested in him. It was because Clara was gaining a piece of him that she'd lost. One that she seriously doubted she could ever get back again. Not with their history.

And it hurt, more than she ever imagined after sixteen years.

CHAPTER 6

"*M*erry Christmas!" Danny called as he walked into the foyer of Atlas and Payton's lakefront home.

"Hey, there you are," Zach Frost said, coming up and giving him a bear hug.

Danny took in the scent of wood and tree needles and smiled. "You just brought them their tree tonight, didn't you?"

"Paying customers first, man," Zach said as he pulled back. "Besides, I'm pretty sure the rock star was off doing a charity concert or some other altruistic thing, so he wasn't here to help me haul it in."

"I was though," Payton said, handing each of them a glass of wine. "I could have helped. In fact, I think we'd have had it up faster than you and Atlas did today."

"You think so?" Atlas draped his arm over his wife's shoulders and grinned down at her. And then before she could answer, he added, "You're probably right. Never underestimate my wife. She's a force of nature."

"I'll remember that." Danny followed them into the house and placed the gift he'd brought under the giant tree that stood in front of the floor-to-ceiling windows that looked out over the lake. He stared at the tree for a long moment, taking his time to remember the year before. To smile at the memory of his grandmother, Georgia, who'd spent her last Christmas in that very house, surrounded by family.

"She's here, you know," Payton said softly as she appeared beside him and slipped her arm through his.

"Has Atlas seen her?" he asked, glancing at his cousin, who was a medium.

"He hasn't said, but it's not necessary. I can feel her presence. Can't you?" She smiled softly up at him. "Ever since I started decorating, she's been on my mind. And I swear I heard her tell me to get her a glass of wine the other day."

Danny laughed. "She would be asking for wine."

"Come on. Dinner's almost ready." Payton led him to the dining room, where Zach and his wife Ilsa were already seated.

"I'm going to go see what mischief Atlas is getting up to in the kitchen," Payton said. "Sit. We'll have dinner on in a minute."

After Payton disappeared into the kitchen, Danny took a seat across from Ilsa.

"No Mia tonight?" Danny asked, referring to Zach and

Ilsa's daughter. She was a sweet preschooler who was the apple of her parents' eyes.

"She's with Holly and Rex tonight. They're making Christmas cookies and overdosing on hot chocolate and marshmallows," Ilsa said with a chuckle. "I told Holly she was going to have to keep her overnight so there was a chance Mia sleeps off all that sugar."

"That's probably a good plan," he agreed, though he could only imagine what it was like to have a child around. Starting a family wasn't something he'd ever thought about after he'd left Marissa. She was the only person he'd ever been able to imagine as the mother of his children.

"It's a brilliant plan. A four-year-old hopped up on sugar is a little demon," Zach said. "A cute one, but a demon nonetheless."

Danny eyed the six place settings. With Mia absent, that meant they only needed five. "Who's our sixth guest?"

Both Zach and Ilsa shrugged.

Ilsa frowned and said, "I told Payton that Mia couldn't make it."

"The place setting isn't for Mia," Payton said as she walked back in the room carrying plates of food. Atlas was right behind her with a couple of bottles of wine. "It's for my friend. She'll be here any minute."

Just as Payton finished placing plates on the table, the doorbell rang.

"That's her!" Payton hurried to get the door.

Atlas held up the wine bottles. "White or red?"

Danny glanced down at the filet and what he knew had to be goat cheese mashed potatoes and said, "Red."

"Good man," Atlas said and proceeded to fill everyone's requests.

When Danny saw that Ilsa went with the white wine, he frowned. With steak? He nearly shuddered at the thought. But then he noted that she had fish with some sort of white wine sauce on her plate. Which meant Payton had gone out of her way to make sure everyone had a meal they really like. He glanced at his cousin, who was still filling wine glasses, and felt a twinge of jealousy. Not because he was a rock star and had more money than should be legal, but because he'd found the love of his life. And by all accounts, she appeared to be the perfect woman. At least when it came to cooking.

Marissa never had been much of a cook. Not back then. But she hadn't been much of a bartender either, and now she was slinging drinks every night and had built quite the following. Danny had loved watching her hands fly while she made cocktails when he was at the bar the night before.

"What are you smiling about?" Ilsa asked in a raised whisper.

"Huh?" he glanced at her and then shrugged. "Just admiring Payton and her hospitality skills."

"No, that's not what that smile was about." Ilsa gave him that mom look that was intended to pry the truth out of one of her kids.

But Danny ignored it. "It's the truth. Look at all the trouble she went through."

"It was no trouble," Payton said, appearing back in the dining room. "You know I like to cook. Just leave room for pie."

Danny turned around to tell her there was always room for pie, but he was struck speechless when he spotted the woman she'd invited. The auburn-haired beauty had an ethereal look about her. Her skin seemed to glow, and her whiskey-colored eyes shone brighter than anyone else's in the room. She wore a long, flowy cream-colored dress and flats that looked like ballet slippers. Nothing about her outfit was weather appropriate.

"Everyone, I want you to meet Sophie," Payton said. "She's in town for the season and has become a regular at the pie shop. Sophie, this is everyone." Payton introduced everyone by name and then seated the otherworldly woman in the chair beside Danny.

Payton and Atlas sat at opposite ends of the table and then Atlas stood to give a toast.

Danny didn't hear a word that Atlas said. He was too busy trying to find some way not to stare at the woman beside him. Not only was she beautiful, but she also had some sort of magical glow that was lighting her from the inside out.

When he noticed she'd put her wine glass to her lips, he glanced around and noted that both his cousins were staring at him with humor in their expressions. They could see that Danny had been transfixed and were just waiting to give him hell about it. He cleared his throat. "So, Sophie, what do you do that brought you to Christmas Grove this holiday season?"

Her smile entranced him, and he was starting to feel like maybe he should step outside for a minute just to clear his head.

But then she spoke, sounding completely normal, and the spell seemed to break. "I'm a project manager of sorts. I'm here to make sure the project we're working on goes smoothly."

"What company do you work for?" Ilsa asked, leaning in and looking almost as transfixed as Danny had.

Good, he thought. At lease he wasn't the only one who appeared to be glitching out when it came to the beautiful stranger.

"Just a small one nobody's ever heard of," Sophie said, tucking a lock of her auburn hair behind her ear. "I'm more interested in hearing about all of you."

That was all it took for each and every one of them to give her a full breakdown of who they were and what they were up to.

Zach had just finished telling her all about the Christmas tree farm when he said, "But I'm not even the most interesting Frost. We also have Atlas, who is a legit rock star, and Danny, who runs a very successful pottery shop. All I do is sell trees."

"Trees that bring joy to hundreds every year," Sophie said.

Zach toasted her with his wine and said, "Yes. That I do."

The woman finally turned to Danny and asked him an unending number of questions about his studio, and she seemed genuinely interested in everything he had to say.

Finally, she said, "I like you, Danny Frost. You should take me on a date tomorrow."

"A date?" he sputtered, completely caught off guard.

"Yes. Breakfast, and then I want to come take classes at your studio. I have always wanted to try pottery. It seems like this is fortuitous, don't you think?"

He didn't think it was fortuitous at all, but he kept that to himself. "I don't know about breakfast. I'm really busy these days—"

"I know. That's what you said," Sophie practically purred at him. "That's why I chose breakfast. For busy people, it's always a great first date. Food is fast and you can have an excuse to leave if it isn't working out. But if it is, you have all day to hang out together. Let's see where that takes us, Danny."

"You can't turn her down now," Zach said.

Atlas just laughed and then backed up Zach by saying, "You're the man, Danny. Take her out, show her a good time, and then bring her by the Christmas Tree Festival at the farm next week."

Danny was ready to kill his cousins, but there was nothing he could do but agree to the date without looking like a major a-hole. "Sophie, would you like to have breakfast with me tomorrow at Candy Canes?"

Her shoulders straightened, and as a pleased smile claimed her face, she said, "I thought you'd never ask."

CHAPTER 7

"*D*on't take this the wrong way," Felicity said as she picked up her mug of plain coffee. "But I think you might still be twelve years old."

Marissa used her middle finger to scratch her nose while she gave her friend a pointed look. "Just because I like chocolate in my pancakes, that doesn't make me twelve."

"It's more like pancakes with your chocolate and yes, I think it does." Felicity picked up a piece of crispy bacon and nibbled on the end.

"Leave her be, City," Clara said. "We're all allowed to like what we like."

"I always knew you were the smarter one of my friends," Marissa said with a cheeky grin. "Prettier and sweeter two."

All three of them laughed. It was Sunday morning, and they were at Candy Canes for their weekly breakfast date.

They'd come a little earlier than normal since they were decorating afterward, and that was why Felicity was a little saltier than usual. Her idea of early on her day off was more like eleven than eight.

Marissa made a big show of forking up a piece of pancake that was loaded with chocolate and then stuffed it in her mouth and made moaning sounds as she chewed.

"Making love to that pancake isn't going to change my mind," Felicity said, causing a new round of laughter.

"You two are the best, you know that, right?" Marissa said, feeling like the luckiest girl in the entire world.

"We know," Felicity said while Clara sobered and stared at the front door.

"What is it?" Marissa asked but didn't need her to answer. The moment she flicked her gaze to the hostess area, she spotted them.

Danny was there, in *her* diner, with the most gorgeous person she'd ever seen in real life. The woman was everything that Marissa was not. She had a waifish build and an interesting, angular face that was highlighted by a beautiful smile and glittering eyes. She wore a white flowy blouse and skirt with gorgeous white boots that were not made for snowy conditions. Where had she come from? Certainly, she wasn't from Christmas Grove. Nobody dressed like that here. And definitely not in December when there was always a chance of snow.

"Wow," Clara said, her voice full of awe. "She looks like she belongs in a mystical garden."

"She looks like she's going to freeze her butt off," Felicity said.

Marissa snorted. Leave it to Felicity to always speak the truth.

"They look really good together," Clara said and then sucked in a sharp breath as she covered her mouth with her hand. "Sorry, Mar. I shouldn't have said that."

"It's fine." Marissa's tone was sharp, indicating that it was anything but fine. She let out a sigh. "Sorry."

"It's all right. I know this is weird for you." Clara leaned over and put her head on Marissa's shoulder. "Some relationships just never let go of a person."

Marissa wrapped and arm around her, giving her a quick hug as she wondered what relationship haunted Clara. She sounded like a woman who completely understood what Marissa was going through, but she'd never said a word about it.

"Uh-oh. Here come the gorgeous shiny people," Felicity muttered.

The hostess made a beeline for their table with Danny and his date following closely behind.

Marissa looked at the empty table right next to them and swallowed a groan. Sure enough, her ex and his ethereal princess were seated right next to them. The woman sat just to the right of Marissa while Danny sat directly across from her.

Danny blinked and then met Marissa's gaze. His eyes flicked to the woman briefly before he grimaced, and Marissa knew then that it was, in fact, a date.

"Hello, Danny. Who's your friend?" she asked, her cheeks aching from the fake smile she'd plastered on.

His expression was wary. Cleary he'd caught on to her

fake cheer. "Marissa, Clara, Felicity, this is Sophie. She's in town for the holiday season."

Sophie's smile reached her eyes as she took in the trio of women. "I've heard so much about each of you. It's just lovely to finally meet you in person."

"You have?" Marissa and Felicity said at the same time.

Clara held out her hand to the woman. "It's lovely to meet you, too. What brings you to Christmas Grove this year, besides the holiday? Do you have family here or…"

"Oh no. My family is spread out all over. I'm here for work, actually." Sophie said cheerfully. "I'm hoping to wrap it up soon." She let her gaze roam over Danny as she added, "I'd love to have time to enjoy everything this charming town has to offer."

Oh no, that wasn't going to happen. Over Marissa's dead body. "It's not really that charming when the rain kicks in. There's nothing pretty about dirty ice and limp Christmas decorations." She turned to Clara. "isn't it supposed to rain next week? I heard something about a front that's supposed to last a week or so. The rivers might even crest. If that's the case, this place will be sandbag city. No place for a tourist to be during the holiday."

"Really?" Clara asked. "I better look at a weather report. If the power goes out, that's a real problem at the studio."

Felicity tried to cover a snort of amusement while Marissa gave Clara a look that said, *seriously?*

"I'm not too worried about a little shower. That's just

nature's way of cleansing the collective. The earth is always beautiful after a decent rain," Sophie said.

Was this chick for real? Marissa wanted to ask Danny what he was doing with a hippy-dippy headcase, but she hadn't quite lost her mind just yet. Instead, she gave Sophie a tight smile and said, "I suggest rain boots."

Sophie smiled at her. "Thank you for the tip."

"Damn, she's good," Felicity whispered so softly that Marissa barely heard her.

Marissa gently nudged her friend with her elbow. Now was not the time. Because she didn't want to sound like a crazy person, she just nodded at the woman and said, "Enjoy your breakfast."

"Thank you." Sophie nodded and then picked up her menu.

Marissa went back to her pancakes, but they'd suddenly lost their appeal, and she spent the next ten minutes pushing them around on her plate. Finally, she put her fork down, admitting defeat.

Felicity raised a questioning eyebrow.

Marissa just shrugged. It was the first time in maybe forever that she hadn't eaten every last bite of her favorite meal. Maybe she just wasn't that hungry.

She chuckled humorlessly to herself. What a liar she was. When it came to her favorite pancakes, hunger didn't have anything to do with it. Obviously she wasn't hungry because Danny and his date had messed up her vibe.

"Care to share with the class?" Clara asked.

Marissa shook her head and waved to the waitress.

"Are you ready for your second hot chocolate?"

Vanessa, the older waitress, asked. Marissa had been coming to the place so long, the woman new her habits backward and forward.

"Not today. But I will take a Bloody Mary," Marissa said.

Vanessa blinked, her painted-on eyebrows rising to her hairline. "Bloody Mary, huh? Today must be special."

"Special. Sure." Marissa tried not to look at Danny but failed and found him staring at her with a troubled expression. She smirked at him and then told Vanessa, "And keep 'em coming."

"You better bring me one, too, then," Felicity said.

"And you?" Vanessa asked Clara.

Clara glanced at her two friends, looking reluctant, but then said, "Sure. Why the heck not?"

"You got it. I sure wish I was partying with you girls today. Looks like you're in for some fun," Vanessa said with a wink.

"Definitely," Felicity agreed as she eyed Danny and his date.

A few minutes later, the Bloody Marys arrived just in time for Sophie to ask when she could get the private pottery classes she'd asked about. Marissa plucked the olives out of her glass and then downed half of it. Before the waitress could even leave, she ordered another.

"That was impressive," Felicity said, giving her a nod of approval. "This is why you're such a fun date."

Danny twisted his head to eye Felicity and then Marissa. His brow was furrowed, and he looked like a concerned dad.

Marissa responded by lifting her glass and taking another long drink.

Danny cleared his throat and said, "I really don't have time for private lessons this month, but I do have group lessons on Sunday afternoons. There's still space if you want to join us today."

"I do," Marissa said without thinking.

Both Sophie and Danny stared at her. Danny had a hint of a smile while Sophie studied her intently. Then she turned back to Danny and said, "That would be lovely. My new friend Marissa and I can get to know each other better."

Marissa gave her a tight smile. They weren't friends. They never would be friends. Not as long as she was dating Danny. Marissa didn't care if she turned out to be Mrs. Freakin' Claus in disguise. Danny was off limits. "Great." Marissa forced her smile again and asked, "What time?"

"What time shall we arrive, Daniel?" Sophie asked.

"It's Danny," Marissa said automatically.

Danny cleared his throat. "I do go by Danny, but I'll answer to either. The class starts at three o'clock. Wear clothes that you don't mind getting dirty."

"Do I need to bring anything else to your shop?" Sophie asked. "What's it called? Pottery something?"

"Pottery Grove," Marissa said, not caring at all that she was eavesdropping and butting in on their conversation. Perhaps the vodka had gone to her head. Or maybe she just needed Sophie to stop trying to make moves on her man. "It's the one with a giant mug painted on the front window."

"Thanks, Marissa," Danny said dryly before speaking to Sophie again. "No, you don't need to bring anything, but you might want to trim your nails and leave the rings at home." He picked up his ice water and took a long sip.

"I can do that," Sophie said. "I'm really looking forward to this."

Vanessa reappeared with Marissa's second Bloody Mary. Then she turned to Danny and Sophie. "Need anything else?"

"Just the check. We have a reservation to take the horseless carriage ride around town in a few minutes," Sophie said. "It should be beautiful with the snow coming down."

"But it's not snowing," Vanessa said, eyeing the front windows where the sun was streaming in as she placed their check on the table.

"It will be." Sophie picked up the check and handed it to Danny.

He placed some bills on the black tray and stood abruptly.

Sophie joined him, and Marissa started in on her second Bloody Mary as she watched them walk out.

Once the pair were safely outside the café, Felicity started to laugh softly until it turned into something close to hysterics. Clara grinned and then suddenly joined her.

"Oh, you think that was funny?" Marissa asked.

"Uh-huh." Felicity nodded and wiped the tears from

beneath her eyes. "You looked like you were ready to scratch her eyes out."

"You're not really going to go take a class with that woman there, are you?" Clara asked after she caught her breath. "That would be next-level crazy, Mar."

"Then someone call the psych ward, 'cause I'm going." Marissa sucked down the rest of her drink, tossed some bills on the table and said, "Let's go. We have decorating to do before I go learn how to make a pot. One that I might be able to drop on that woman's head if she doesn't stay away from—" She abruptly closed her mouth. What was she saying? Danny wasn't hers to fight for. But that didn't mean she wouldn't be at that class right at three p.m.

"Danny?" Felicity filled in for her. "If Sophie hasn't figured out by now that she's gonna have to go through you to get that man, then I kinda feel a little sorry for her."

Marissa didn't answer. She just got up and said, "Come on. There's decorating to do and nog to drink." She hiccuped on the word *drink* and let out a small laugh as she patted her chest.

"Maybe you should pace yourself today," Clara said, taking her friend by the arm. As they walked out, Marissa stumbled slightly and Clara shook her head, mumbling, "It's a good thing I drove today."

"You're not drunk, too?" Marissa asked, looking her up and down.

"No, sweetie. I only had a few sips. Now let's get in the car and get our merry on, okay?"

"Yeah, okay." Marissa reached for the driver's door

handle, but before she could get the door open, Clara guided her to the back seat.

"Dang, girl. That vodka hit you hard," Clara said. "Usually you're much better at holding your liquor."

"I think Vanessa made them doubles," Felicity said as she climbed into the front passenger seat. "That would mean our girl here drank four in like ten minutes. That's a lot, even for her."

"Whoa boy. Yep. Okay, let's get her home and sobered up before she goes throwing mud around Danny's shop."

Felicity nodded. "That just means more nog for me."

CHAPTER 8

*W*hat in the world had Danny Frost gotten himself into? First, he'd gone on the ill-advised date with Sophie. Sure, she was beautiful and had a mystical allure that seemed to just draw people to her, but Danny mostly just found her exhausting. For the two hours they were on the horseless carriage ride, she kept asking him about his inner deepest thoughts and then pivoted to game show questions like, 'if you could take your first date anywhere, where would it be?'

It seemed like she'd read a how-to book on dating and was checking off some sort of list. He couldn't have been less interested in her if she were the last single female in the entire state.

What had interested him though, was breakfast. If he'd known that Marissa was going to be there, he'd have definitely pushed for a different place. He probably should have just steered clear altogether since he knew the establishment meant a lot to her, but there were only a few choices in town for breakfast, and he hadn't wanted to take his date to a coffee shop. It was just his dumb luck that he'd chosen the day that she was there.

This was his cousins' fault. If they hadn't pushed him into the date with Sophie, he wouldn't have been there at all. But he'd been backed into a corner, and if he hadn't asked Sophie out, he'd have looked like a grade-A jackass. Maybe he would anyway when he told her he wasn't interested, but it had to be done sooner rather than later.

Danny just wasn't into Sophie at all. He'd known that last night before the public pressure campaign, but he'd agreed to take her out and had tried to keep an open mind. By the time she exclaimed that Christmas Grove was the perfect place to raise kids, he'd been completely done.

He was so over it he'd even considered canceling the pottery class that afternoon just to make sure he didn't have to see Sophie again. But Marissa had said she was coming, and he just couldn't bring himself to cancel and miss out on whatever that fiasco would bring.

Maybe he was a little bit evil, but Marissa's jealous display that morning had amused him. It had also sparked a light of hope deep in his consciousness that maybe, just maybe she didn't hate him and all her animosity was because she still hadn't let go of him. Not completely. And that possibility made his heart beat just a little bit faster.

He'd tried to tell himself that it didn't matter. That they'd broken up for a very good reason and picking up where they left off was impossible. But still... He couldn't quiet the voice in his head that told him she was his person. That she always had been and always would be despite whether they were together or not.

He got each of the pottery wheel stations ready to go with the supplies they'd need and then went into the gallery to wait for his students.

Kathy and Jill, a mom and her teenage daughter who'd been to his group class before were the first to show up. "Danny!" Jill, the teenager, cried as she ran over and threw her arms around him. "I just know I'm going to get the perfect mug today. And once it's fired, I can give it to my dad for Christmas."

He pulled away and smiled down at her. "Then let's make sure you end up with a great one today, okay? Don't be afraid to ask for help if you need it."

She frowned. "I hope I don't need help. I want to make it all by myself."

"That's fine, too, but if you need advice on technique, I'm here, okay?" On any other day, this was maybe his most favorite part of his job. He really liked sharing the joy of his craft with other people. And when they went away feeling joyful and triumphant, it soothed that place in his soul, telling him that he was making a difference. Maybe it was a small one in the grand scheme of things, but it was very important to him to bring that energy into the world.

"Go on into the back and pick your stations. I'll be in as soon as the rest of the students get here," Danny told the pair.

Kathy mouthed *thanks* and then the two of them went into the studio.

The door swung open, and Marissa walked in. She was wearing ripped blue jeans and a faded old sweatshirt that he was certain she'd had since high school. "Does your sweatshirt say *Cougars* on it?" Danny asked, staring intently at the faded lettering.

"Up here, buddy," she said, waving a hand at him and then pointing to her eyes.

"What?" He blinked and then realized the faded letters were right across her bustline. He felt his cheeks heat and stuttered when he said, "S-sorry. That's not—never mind. I was just trying to read the words on your sweatshirt."

She smirked. "I know. I was just messing with you. Yes, it says *Cougars*. It's from high school. I'd say it's vintage, but it's so faded now I think it's just old. I usually wear it when I'm working in my yard, so I put it on for our annual decorating party. By the time we were done trimming my house and the one that Clara and Felicity share, I was nearly late, so I just wore it. I figured you'd appreciate the school spirit."

Appreciate? No. All it did was make him remember her wearing it all those years ago. And how he'd dreamed of taking it off her right up until the day he'd finally gotten his wish. He clamped down on that memory hard. Now was not the time to be reminiscing about *that*.

"Right," he said, running a hand through his short hair. "We're just waiting for—"

"You haven't started without me, have you?" Sophie glided into the gallery, wearing white flowing pants and a matching shirt. To top off her highly inappropriate outfit, she'd worn white high heels.

"What are you wearing?" Marissa blurted. "You do realize this is a pottery class, right? We will literally be playing with clay."

Sophie glanced down at herself. "What's wrong with this? I thought I was supposed to wear something comfortable that I didn't mind if it got dirty."

"You were," Danny said. "I meant like jeans and a T-shirt. Or a button-down shirt you'd only wear while painting your house. Not... this." He wasn't even sure what to call her ensemble. It looked like something he'd seen in a movie where two women wore linen pants and tunics to stay cool on a hot southern day while sipping sweet tea and repeating town gossip.

"This is fine. It's old and I never wear it. Now, where do we start?" Sophie asked.

Danny shook his head. He guessed he wasn't too surprised. So far everything that Sophie had worn had that rich bohemian vibe. It seemed insane to him that she wanted to take the chance of getting mud splattered all over her, but it was her decision.

"Come on." Danny waved for the two women to join him in the pottery studio.

He waved at the pottery wheels that were lined up and said, "Grab an apron and then pick a seat. Doesn't matter which one."

"Where are you sitting?" Sophie asked Danny as her heels echoed off the cement floor.

"At the end to demonstrate and then I'll be walking

around, answering questions and helping wherever I'm needed."

He watched as Marissa took the wheel closest to where he'd be demonstrating.

But when Sophie spotted her already getting comfortable on the short stool, she walked over and loomed over Marissa. "Would you mind moving? I have trouble hearing instructions, and I do better when I sit in the front of the class."

"This isn't a classroom," Marissa said, making no effort to move.

"Yes it is." Sophie pointed to the stool next to them. "That's a perfectly good space. I don't see why you can't just move down one."

"Maybe because I—" Marissa started in a sharp tone and then abruptly stopped when she saw Kathy and Jill starting at them. Then without a word, she moved over one space.

If Danny had been on the fence about dating Sophie, that horrific display of self-entitlement would have told him everything he needed to know. "Okay, there's just the five of us today. Me, two newbies, and two repeat offenders."

Kathy and Jill chuckled softly.

"Thank you! Finally, someone appreciates my humor." He saluted Jill, making her beam.

"I'm sorry, Danny," Sophie said in a sickeningly sweet voice. "I know you're trying to hype us up, but I don't need all that. I have a schedule to keep today, and if we don't get moving, I'm going to be late."

"Late? For what?" Danny asked.

"Her Wicked Witch of the West meeting," Marissa muttered.

"Wicked Witch?" Sophie let out a soft chuckle. "That's a new one. Usually it's more along the lines of Tink."

Marissa grimaced but didn't offer an apology. While the woman seemed magical earlier while they'd been having breakfast, now she just seemed like an entitled tourist, and Marissa prayed that Danny saw through her strange facade.

"Let's just get started, shall we?" Danny sat on the stool at the end of the two rows and started talking about the properties of clay, why water was used in throwing, and how to center the clay in the middle of the wheel. He gave a demonstration, making it look very easy, and then he moved on to showing us how to throw a pot. When he was done, he leaned back and said, "Okay, your turn. Make me a pot using the techniques I just showed you."

Everyone got to work. Jill and Kathy dove right in, and Danny was not surprised when Jill had made the mug she'd wanted perfectly.

"You're a natural," Danny said, giving her a high five. Then he moved on to Sophie, who somehow had a bunch of clay handprints on her apron but had managed to keep every inch of her white outfit completely clean. *Maybe Marissa was right and she was some kind of witch.*

"Am I doing this right?" Marissa asked him as she tried to raise the walls of her pot.

"Almost," Danny said as he stood behind her and eyed her technique. "You need to push harder with your fingers on the inside and just guide it with the fingers on the outside of the wall."

Marissa tried to emulate what he'd said, but the pot was just getting wider and wider, instead of taller. "I'm clearly not understanding something."

Danny glanced over at Sophie. Her pot looked perfect. It was pretty enough to rival even Danny's best.

"She's a ringer," Marissa said. "I don't think she really needed lessons."

Danny agreed. It wasn't normal for someone to pick up this craft right out of the gate. He turned his attention back to Marissa. Her pot was quickly becoming a lost cause. "Do you mind if I sit behind you and guide your hands with my hands?" he asked her.

Marissa startled for a second and then quickly nodded. "Yes, please."

"You got it." Danny was nervous as he pulled his chair over and positioned it behind her. The anticipation of having her in his arms made his hands shake, so instead of putting them right on her hands to steady her project, he ran his hands down her arms first.

That was a mistake. A huge one.

Because suddenly he didn't care about pottery, his store, this class. He just wanted her in his arms and the rest of the world be damned.

"Danny?" Sophie said as she concentrated on her piece. "I think you're going to be impressed by this."

"I'm in the middle of something," he shot back, unwilling to interrupt this moment for anything in the world.

He slipped his fingers over Marissa's and for a brief moment, they held them there, intertwining their fingers. His eyes were closed, and he was taking in every single second of touching the woman he'd ached for far too long.

"Son of a—"

Slap!

Danny sat stunned as he watched the wet clay drip off Marissa's nose. The wet clay that had come from Sophie's wheel. "Oh, oops!," Sophie said and then let out a laugh as if she hadn't almost taken Marissa's eye out.

"Are you okay?" he asked Marissa. She wasn't screaming and threatening to sue anyone, so that was a good sign.

"I'm fine," she said and got up to rinse the clay off her face. The moment she sat back down, Sophie reached over and grabbed her arm. "Look, I did it!"

The pot was very good for a first try. Hell, it would stand up to any of his instructor's work. He narrowed his eyes at Sophie. "This isn't the first time you've done pottery."

"It's not?" Sophie asked, putting on an air of innocence.

Danny just shook his head and walked away. He wanted nothing to do with someone who was that experienced but still managed to hit Marissa in the face with a very wet piece of clay.

Marissa was staring at Sophie, and then as if a black force of evil had walked right into the studio and possessed her, Marissa stood up and smeared her completely covered-in-mud hands right down the back of Sophie's pristine white shirt.

Danny was rendered speechless, but not for long when Sophie threw her hands up in a V.

"Finally! Victory at last." Sophie grinned at Jill and Kathy. "Do you mind giving us some privacy? There are things I need to discuss with Danny and Marissa."

"I think that's for the best," Kathy said, tugging her daughter along after her. "Danny," she said on the way out, "I think we'll be doing private lessons from now on."

"Sure, Kathy. I'm sorry about that. I had no idea any of this would happen."

"I should hope not," Kathy said with a sniff of impatience. "It's just not fun when other people are desperate for your attention."

Danny walked her and Jill through the store and then returned to the studio to find Marissa with her arms crossed over her chest, demanding to know why Sophie felt it was necessary to ruin everyone's experiences.

"Not everyone's," she said, lifting her head as if she were proud of herself. "Yours specifically." Her voice was full of glee.

"Mine! Why? What did I ever do to you?" Marissa demanded.

"Nothing. But that's not relevant. What you should be asking is why I'm here."

Danny stepped in between them and said, "Fine. I'll bite. Why are you here?"

Sophie sobered immediately. "To right a wrong that was committed sixteen years ago."

"Sixteen years ago?" Marissa and Danny cried at the same time.

She smiled. "Yes. Sixteen. Marissa, Danny, it's your lucky day."

"How's that?" Danny asked.

"Because," she said, looking almost gleeful, "I'm going to give you the tools to break that curse that's been hanging over your heads."

"Curse? What curse?" Marissa asked.

"The one that scared your husband away all those years ago. I'm here to make sure it doesn't happen again."

Danny stared at her as if she were an alien. His arms were crossed over his chest, and he wanted to throw her out. But he couldn't, not when she was saying things about a curse. A curse he hadn't known about and was skeptical it actually existed. "If you're here to help, then what was the date about? And the childish clay fight? If you had something to say, you should have just said it."

"I needed to see if the passion was still there," Sophie said and then mimed polishing her nails on her lapel. "It is. In spades. The two of you will be naked together by nightfall."

Danny took a long look at Marissa and said, "Gods, I hope so."

CHAPTER 9

*D*anny *wanted her in his bed?* Marissa stared at her ex in utter shock. What was happening? She met his gaze, wishing she could see what was going on in his mind. "Danny?"

He walked over to her, grabbed both of her hands, and held them to his chest. "The last thing I ever wanted to do was hurt you. If I thought there was a way to stay and keep you safe, I would have. I just need you to know that."

The anger that had lived inside her ever since he'd disappeared from her life roared its ugly head, and she pulled her hands out of his and stepped back. "It doesn't matter if you didn't want to hurt me. The fact is you did. You shattered me, Danny."

"And that's why it's your lucky day that I'm here. It's time to undo all that damage," Sophie said, grinning at them.

"You can't fix everything just like that, Sophie," Marissa barked at her.

"Actually, you'd be amazed by what a sugar plum fairy can do," Sophie said.

"Sugar plum fairy?" Marissa asked. "What the hell does that mean?"

"I'm a sugar plum fairy, and I'm here to make your Christmas wishes come true." She did an elaborate bow as if she'd just presented Marissa with a seven-figure check. "You have to know about sugar plum fairies. We show up during the holidays and help people whose lives have gone off track. Like fairy godmothers at Christmas time."

She's lost her mind, Marissa thought. That's all there was to it. Should she call 911? Social services? Who had the power to get this woman some help? "I think maybe we should all just slow down and take a breath here."

"Sure. A lot of people need a minute after I introduce the real me. I'm used to it." Sophie leaned against a clay-covered counter, seemingly unconcerned with further dirtying her outfit.

Marissa supposed it didn't matter since it was already ruined, but it wasn't what she would have chosen to do. When no one said anything, Marissa walked over to Danny and whispered, "I think we need to get her some help. This isn't normal."

Danny pressed his lips together into a thin line and then shook his head. "I'm not ruling it out, but give me a minute."

Sophie chuckled to herself. "If I had a dollar for every time someone said I needed help, I'd be driving my dream car. Have you ever experienced the thrill of a twin-turbo V8 Aston Martin?"

"I can't say I have," Danny said.

She pressed her fingertips to her lips and kissed them before exclaiming, "Just divine. One hundred percent 10 out of 10. Can't recommend enough."

"I'll keep that in mind," he said dryly. "But for now, tell me about this curse. What do you mean you can break the curse?"

"Oh, *I* can't break the curse. Only you can. But I can tell you how."

"How?" Danny asked, and his earnest tone concerned Marissa. He didn't honestly believe anything Sophie was saying, did he? Because as far as Marissa could tell, she was out of her mind.

"She doesn't know anything, Danny," Marissa said. "Sugar plum fairies aren't real. They're just made-up holiday tales. Don't let her suck you into her fantasy."

"Not real?" Sophie pushed herself off the bench, held one finger up, and then moved it around in a clockwise motion. Magic suddenly appeared in the form of glittering light as it wrapped around her from head to toe. Her clay-stained white outfit suddenly morphed into a cream-colored flowy dress, and her stilettos turned into sparkling ankle boots. All evidence of the clay was gone, and she once again looked just like the ethereal being that had walked into Candy Canes that morning with Danny. "Now you see where the Tink thing comes from."

"That was… impressive," Danny said.

"Not really." Marissa narrowed her eyes at Sophie. "I

know more than one witch who can wield their magic like that. That doesn't make you a sugar plum fairy. It just means you have magic, which isn't exactly in short supply in Christmas Grove." She glanced at Danny. "We can't trust her."

"You have no reason not to," Sophie reasoned. "I'm going to tell you how to break that curse. What you do with the information is up to you."

"Why would you tell us? What's in it for you?" Marissa asked, unable to shake her distrust. She wasn't even sure she believed there was a curse, much less that they had to figure out how to break it. She'd been living a good life in Christmas Grove the past five years. If she'd been cursed, wouldn't she know that?

"Points for my sugar plum wings of course," Sophie said as if that was obvious. "Your case is worth a lot because you've been apart for so long. If I can help you two get back together, I'll be promoted and finally get my wings."

Marissa glanced around, looking for the hidden cameras. She was being punked, right? Someone would surely pop out and try to get her to sign a release for their ridiculous television show, and then she'd have to restrain herself from kicking their ass.

"Once I have my wings," Sophie continued, "I'll be able to join the task force that goes after fallen fairies. The ones who do things like curse happy couples just for spite."

"There are fallen fairies?" Marissa asked, unable to

help herself. While she didn't think she believed a word Sophie was saying, she had to admit she was curious.

"Sadly, yes. One of them cursed your relationship. I'm basically the cleanup crew."

"Sixteen years later?" Marissa was incredulous. Sophie was sounding more and more like she needed to see a mental health professional.

She nodded. "Unfortunately, it took me a long time to search out all the curses my sister cast on people, and fixing them takes longer than casting them. It's been a long road. And then I had to find out if you were up for the task. Make sure you really are meant to be together. Because if not, then it wouldn't be worth it. If you never wanted to see each other again, the effort would be wasted."

Danny held up his hand. "Wait, your sister cast a curse?"

"Yes. She fell in love with you and was mad you were taken. Do you remember Patience? She was in your Accounting 101 class. You two were in a study group for a while."

Danny's eyes went wide, and then he scowled. "Patience did this to us?"

Sophie nodded. "Yes. She cast what's known as Cupid's Curse. Basically, it causes obstacles in relationships. One never really knows how that is going to manifest itself. Sometimes it's things like a difficult mother-in-law. Other times it's an ex causing trouble. And then there's the tried-and-true job transfer that's three thousand miles away. For you two, it was bad luck that turned dangerous." She stared pointedly at Danny. "And Patience sent you to a mage who told you that you were the cause of all of Marissa's bad luck. That your visions were manifesting the accidents and the only way to help her was to put distance between you."

Marissa sucked in a sharp breath. "Danny?"

He met her gaze, pain shining back at her.

"You left because a mage told you that you were hurting me?" she asked, needing to hear it from him.

"Yes. I kept getting visions of you getting hurt, and each incident was getting worse and worse, so I was seeking help on how to change things. Patience said she knew a mage in town who could help. I went to her. She knew about my visions and your near misses and told me that our energies didn't mix. It was because of me that you kept getting hurt. The only way to stop it was to separate." He ground his teeth together and sucked in a deep breath before continuing. "I tried to ignore her advice, but then you were almost hit by that taxi and it scared me to death. I left the next day. And when the visions stopped and I learned you hadn't had any more near misses, I just knew that mage was right, so I talked to the lawyer. Marissa, I couldn't live with myself if you were hurt when I could do something to stop it."

Marissa's heart rate sped up as heat rushed to her face. Her heart was beating against her rib cage, and she suddenly felt like she was just going to explode. Her mouth worked soundlessly as her words got stuck in her throat. Finally she sputtered and said, "You... you didn't tell me? You saw a mage and didn't think I deserved to know what was said? You made that decision without including me? How dare you, Danny Frost? How. Dare. You."

Danny took a step back, blinking and holding his hands up in surrender. "Marissa, I was just trying to—"

"No!" Marissa cried, cutting him off. "I don't want to hear your excuses! I was your wife. Your best friend. And you took it upon yourself to decide our lives with zero input from me! Who do you think you are?"

"Someone who loves you more than anything else in this world!" he shot back, taking a step forward. "You think that was easy for me? Do you think I haven't spent every single day of these last sixteen years second guessing my decision? Wanting to look for you? Wanting to tell you? Wanting to wrap you in my arms and make you mine again? Do you have any idea what it's like to never be able to move on from a decision you made when you were just nineteen years old? I was a nineteen-year-old who was too scared that if I told you any of it I'd never have the strength and courage to leave you. Be angry if you want. Scream at me. Tell me how wrong I was. Trust me when I say that it's nothing I haven't already inflicted on myself."

Danny squeezed his eyes shut and took a step back, shaking his head. "I'm sorry. You didn't deserve that."

Marissa didn't care. There was only one thing running through her mind. "You said you love me."

"Yeah, so?" He looked at her with confusion in his gorgeous dark green eyes.

"Present tense." Her voice was shaking.

He let out a soft laugh. "Yeah. Present tense, Marissa. The love I have for you never goes away."

She took a half step forward but then froze. What was she going to do when she reached him? Hug him? Kiss him? Throw herself at him? Any of those actions would be a huge mistake. She'd just learned a lot of information that she'd been missing for sixteen years. She needed to process what it all meant.

Danny's eyes turned glassy as he seemed to stare over her shoulder at nothing.

Marissa stiffened and waited. She'd witnessed that look many, many times before. He was having a vision, and there was no way to know if it was good or bad.

He suddenly shook his head and then stared intently at Marissa before he reached for her and yanked her into his arms. There was a loud crash just behind her, and she felt something slam against her right calf, making her wince.

Danny spun her around as he picked her up and carried her to a chair near the door that led to the gallery. After gently easing her down, he knelt before her, looked up, and asked, "Are you all right?"

"I'm fine. What fell?" she asked, trying to see past him.

"A shelf with a bunch of glazes. The supports gave out and almost fell on your head," he said, his nostrils flaring as he turned to stare at the scene of the crime.

"It's the curse," Sophie said with a nod, her voice cheerful. "That's going to keep happening until you manage to break the hold it has on both of you."

Marissa wanted to scream at her. Lives had been

ruined. Turning this into whatever game she was playing was just cruel.

Danny tightened his hand around Marissa's as he asked Sophie, "How do I break the curse?"

"You have to do it together," she said, and her tone was softer and slightly sympathetic. "It won't be easy, but unless you do the work, you'll both be miserable. Trust me." Her expression turned sad. "I've been there."

Marissa stared at the woman, horrified as all the ethereal glow that had surrounded her seemed to dissipate, leaving just an older, wrinkled lady standing before them, wearing a cotton dress and orthopedic shoes.

Sophie glanced down at herself and muttered a curse before meeting Marissa's gaze. "This will be you in twenty years if you refuse to do the work to heal your broken heart." She pressed her fingertip to her temple, unleashing another round of sparkling magic. Just like that, she was the gorgeous fairy again, her eyes sparkling and not a wrinkle in sight. "Loneliness ages you quickly, Marissa. I hope you take my warning to heart."

"I'm in my thirties!" Marissa exclaimed.

"I know, dear." Sophie wrapped her fingers around Marissa's and then grabbed Danny's hand too. "The way to break the curse is to spend as much time together as possible. You need to learn to trust each other again. When that happens, the spell will be broken."

Before either of them could say another word, Sophie vanished into thin air.

CHAPTER 10

"You don't really believe any of that, do you?" Marissa asked as she inched toward the door to the gallery.

Danny wanted to reach out and stop her. He wanted to pull her into his arms and never let go. But she was clearly spooked, and he thought if he got any closer she might bolt. "Yes, I do."

Marissa balled her hands into fists as irritation radiated off her. "I am *not* going to look ninety in twenty years if I don't forgive you."

That wasn't what Sophie had implied, but Danny was smart enough to keep his thoughts to himself. "Not with medical advances." He gave her a small smile and then felt his head and eyesight go fuzzy the way they always did when a vision was bearing down on him. Then the image of Marissa tripping over a large pot in his gallery flashed in his consciousness.

The vision was gone just as quickly as it arrived, but he always needed a moment to get reoriented.

"What did you see?" Marissa asked him.

"Be careful of the large pot to the right of the door when you go back into the gallery. If you knock it over, you're going to end up falling and cutting your leg deep enough that you'll need stitches."

"That's two visions in less than five minutes," she said and then stared at him as if waiting for some sort of answer.

"Yes. It was like this toward the end when we were married. It's why I sought out help." Frustration was getting the better of him, and he had to keep his attitude in check so that he didn't snap at her. The visions really took it out of him sometimes, especially when they were about her. All the memories would come roaring back, and then he was left with a deep-seated sadness.

Marissa's shoulders sagged as she leaned against the wall. Her eyes were red, and it looked like she was holding back tears. "I wish you wouldn't have kept any of that from me. But right now, I can't spend more time with you. I need... I don't know what I need. Time to process this, I guess."

"I understand," he said, knowing there was no other answer.

"Do you really?" she asked, peering at him as if she were trying to look into his soul.

"Of course I do." This time he let his irritation show. She was acting like she was the only one who'd been hurt. If Sophie was right, Danny had just learned that he'd left his entire life behind, based on a lie. It was one hell of a pill to swallow.

She frowned. "Okay then. I should go." Marissa hesitated a long moment before she turned and walked through the door leading to the gallery.

Danny sat on one of the stools and buried his throbbing head in his hands, digging his fingers into his scalp, trying to ease the ache.

Crash!

"Dammit!" Danny jumped up and burst through the door to find Marissa standing next to the pot he'd warned her about. It was in pieces on the floor, but one glance at her leg confirmed that she'd avoided getting cut.

"I'm so sorry," she said, kneeling down to try to gather the broken ceramic pieces. "I remembered your vision at the last moment and grabbed the door handle to keep from falling. Unfortunately, I couldn't save your pot." She stopped gathering the broken pieces and reached into her bag, pulling out her wallet. "How much is it? I'll pay for it."

"No way," Danny said, waving the idea away. "And don't worry about cleaning it up. I don't want you to cut yourself on the sharp edges. I'll broom it up. It happens. I can always make another one. I'm just glad you're okay."

She sat back on her heels and looked up at him, her expression slightly defeated. "I'm sorry, Danny."

He walked over to her, holding out a hand.

She took it and pulled herself up.

"There's nothing to be sorry for."

Marissa shook her head. "I should have listened to you.

I was just overwhelmed and hurrying out when I should have been paying more attention after your vision."

He squeezed her hand. "Like I said. It's all right."

They stood there like that, holding hands, not saying a word until a tall, leggy, raven-haired woman pulled the door open and froze when she saw the pottery shards on the floor. "Oh gosh. That's not good."

Marissa dropped Danny's hand and stepped out of the way, leaving his fingers cold. "Just a small accident," she mumbled.

Danny gave the woman a smile. He recognized her as Payton's former boss. They'd met at Payton and Atlas's wedding the year before. She owned the newest inn in town, The Enchanted, and had been in before to inquire about specialty mugs that included their logo. "Olivia, it's nice to see you. Come on in and take a look around while I sweep that up."

"I better go," Marissa said. "I'll... talk to you later."

Danny nodded at her and tried to ignore the dull ache in his chest as she walked away from him.

"Rough day?" Olivia asked, her tone full of sympathy.

"You could say that," he said but then pasted on a smile. "The joys of running a retail operation, right? Let me get that broom."

"I've got it." Olivia pointed at the broken mess but then dropped her hand and asked, "Where is your garbage bin?"

He walked behind the cashier counter and placed the small bin where she could see it.

"Perfect." Olivia pointed at the broken mess, crooked

her finger, and then turned and pointed to the bin. A wind picked up, swirling the mess into a spiral off the floor, and then every last piece of the broken pot shot right into the bin.

Danny walked over to where the mess had been and let out a low whistle. "That was impressive. If you didn't have an inn to run, you could clean up in the housekeeping department."

She let out a guffaw and shook her head. "That was a terrible pun."

He chuckled. "Fair enough. Thank you. I appreciate your help."

"Sure." Olivia walked over to the wall of mugs and plucked a midnight blue one with a white rim off the shelf and said, "I've got an idea in mind. Do you think we can modify this a bit for the custom mugs we talked about?"

"Absolutely." Danny made a conscious effort to brush off the events of the afternoon so that he could focus on Olivia as he got out a pen and paper. "Shoot."

By the time they worked out what was possible that matched Olivia's vision, Danny was feeling almost normal again. Delving into his creative energy had always helped to center him when he was going through something stressful. They agreed on a prototype, and when Danny walked her to the door, he said, "Thanks for the opportunity to work on this project with you. I'm really looking forward to it."

"Thank you, Danny. I'm very excited. If they go over well with our guests, hopefully it will be lucrative for both of us." She stepped out the door, waved, and said, "Merry Christmas!"

"Same to you." He shut the door, glanced at the clock, turned the closed sign, and locked up. Everything inside of him wanted to head to Sleighed, to see Marissa, to spend time with her just as Sophie had said. But he knew if he pushed her she'd bolt. So instead, he went back into his studio and forced himself to sit at his pottery wheel.

But after ten minutes, he gathered up the ruined pot, formed the clay into a ball, and tossed it back onto his work bench. His mind was too busy racing. Working wasn't going to be an option. Not tonight.

He locked up, stopped off at home to shower, feed Bells and give her some love, and then got back in his 4Runner and headed to the one place that he thought might give him some peace.

Half a dozen cars were parked in the lot in front of the Frost Family Tree Farm. Christmas music was playing from the speakers set up throughout the property, and a trio of kids were running around tossing snowballs at each other. The cheer instantly made the dark cloud hanging over Danny's head dissipate. It was hard to be a Grinch when everyone was so full of Christmas spirit.

"Danny, hey man," Zach said, spotting him when he walked through the gate into the clearing. He was behind a table that was set up with a hot chocolate station as well as Christmas cookies and various pies. "Are you here for a tree?"

After hesitating for just a moment, Danny nodded. He hadn't come to the farm for that, but now that he was here, he thought it was just the thing he needed to cheer up his apartment for the season. "Nothing too big. There's not a lot of space in my apartment, but it'd be nice to decorate for the holiday."

"What about the gallery? We can deliver one there, too," Zach said as he handed a woman a cup of hot chocolate.

"Sure. Why not?" Danny walked over to the table and grabbed a reindeer-shaped cookie. After he took a bite, he asked, "How much?"

"I don't charge family." Zach emerged from behind the table and wrapped an arm around Danny's shoulders. "Now, tell me how your date with Sophie went. Will she be your date at the family Christmas gathering this year?"

Danny let out a bark of laughter. "Hardly. Do you know what she is?"

"*What* she is?" Zach asked as he paused to look at his cousin. They were standing in front of a room of trees that couldn't have been more than five feet tall. "I know *who* she is. One of Payton's friends who is here for the season. As for *what* she is, are you implying she's a fugitive or something?" he asked with a laugh.

"That certainly would be less complicated," Danny deadpanned.

Zach frowned at him. "What's going on, Danny?"

"Apparently Sophie is a sugar plum fairy and is here to help me and Marissa repair our relationship." Danny waited a beat, and when Zach didn't say anything, he added, "I told you a fugitive would be simpler."

"A sugar plum fairy?" Zach asked, looking dubious.

"You mean like someone who is sent to earth to bring joy?"

"Sort of. I guess. I don't know for sure if that's exactly right," Danny said, frowning. "She said it's her job to make Christmas wishes come true and to right the wrongs of fallen fairies. She said her sister cursed me and Marissa and that's why our marriage fell apart."

"I thought your marriage fell apart because of your visions," Zach said, looking concerned.

"Well, yeah, but that was part of the curse. Sophie says the only way to break the curse is to spend as much time as possible with Marissa, but she's not interested. I'm just... I don't know, man. It turns out that I was fed bad information back then, and it blew up my life. I'm not sure there's any fixing it now." He ran a hand through his hair, wanting to scream. Maybe coming here to see Zach had been the wrong idea. "I should go. I didn't mean to dump any of this on you."

When Danny started to walk away, his cousin grabbed his arm, stopping him. "Wait. Come with me."

Danny didn't ask questions. He just followed his cousin, ignoring the activity around him. He was tired of trying to process the events of the day. Soon enough, Zach led him into the outbuilding that served as his office.

Without a word, Zach reached into his desk and pulled out a bottle of whiskey and two shot glasses. After pouring them each a shot, he held one up and said, "Here's to taking the first step into the rest of your life."

Danny eyed the shot and then his cousin. "What if it doesn't turn out the way I hope?"

"There aren't any guarantees in life, man. But imagine having the opportunity to undo a mistake you made years ago and not doing everything in your power to make it happen."

"How do you know I think it was a mistake?" There wasn't a lot in Danny's life that he regretted, and until a few hours ago, he hadn't regretted leaving Marissa. He'd desperately wished things could have been different, but he'd also never regretted keeping her safe.

"Dude, it's obvious every time you look at her." He held his shot glass up again.

Danny nodded once, touched his glass to Zach's, and downed the amber liquid, vowing that one way or another, he'd do everything he could to break the curse that had kept them apart for far too many years.

"Good man. Now, let's go get you those trees," Zach said.

Danny nodded, but when they got outside, he asked, "Do you mind if I help out here for a while first? I think a little holiday cheer might be just what I need to clear my head."

"Help?" Zach chuckled. "We can always use help. How about loading trees for the customers after they check out?"

"Perfect." Danny followed his cousin out to the parking lot where a woman and her preteen son were trying to load a tree on top of their SUV. Danny walked up to them. "Do you mind if I help?"

The woman glanced at him, let out a sigh of relief, and

said, "Thank the Christmas gods. My arms are killing me, and I haven't even tied the first knot yet."

Danny gave her a sympathetic smile. "Don't worry. I'll have this done in no time." Since the tree was already on the roof, he showed her son how and where to tie the rope, and once it was secure, he tapped the roof, letting the woman know they were done.

She leaned out the window, holding out a tip. "Thank you for your trouble."

"You don't need to do that," he said, trying to refuse the money. He really was there just trying to keep his mind off his own troubles.

"I insist," she said. "If I'd had to do that myself, I'm sure it would have ended up swimming in the river the first time I took a corner. You're a life saver."

He took the cash, pocketed it, and wished her and her family a Merry Christmas. By the end of the night, he had a pocket full of cash that he stuffed into the tip jar near the hot chocolate station. He got one of the five foot trees and then went home to Bells, determined to find the Christmas spirit. He was going to need it if he was going to convince Marissa to believe in sugar plum fairies.

When he drifted off to sleep that night, all he saw in his mind was him and Marissa and a sable-colored dog in a porch swing, watching as snow drifted down on a nearby tree that was covered in twinkling lights.

CHAPTER 11

$\mathcal{M}$arissa knocked once on Felicity and Clara's door, and without waiting for them to answer, she barged in. "I hope everyone is decent!"

"Marissa?" Clara called before suddenly appearing in the living room. She was wearing a cow print apron and had a red Christmas bow tied around her dark ponytail. "I thought you'd be at Sleighed tonight."

"It's Kira's night." Kira Andrews was the other bartender that typically covered the two nights that Marissa didn't work.

"Right. Of course." Clara gestured for Marissa to follow her into the kitchen. "I'm making Christmas cookies. Want some nog?"

Marissa shook her head as she followed her friend into her kitchen. "No, but I'll have a cup of coffee if you have any Irish cream."

"We do. You know where to find it," she said as she went back to mixing the flour into her batter.

"You're an angel," Marissa said as she made her coffee and broke out the Irish cream. "You're never going to believe what happened at the pottery lesson today."

Clara glanced up at her and frowned as her gaze roamed over her friend. "What in the world? Did you roll around on the floor or something? You look like you got into a fight with the clay and it won."

"I got into a fight with Sophie, and *I* won," Marissa insisted.

"What?" Clara put her mixer down and stared at her friend. "Tell me that you and that woman did not have a mud fight."

Marissa couldn't help it. She let out a bark of laughter but then quickly sobered. "Sorry. We did end up in a mud fight, sort of, I guess. But she started it."

"Oh, that's much better," Clara said dryly. "What did Danny do?"

"Stopped the class. Obviously. But that's not what I need to tell you. Sophie isn't just some woman who is spending her holidays in Christmas Grove. She's here to try to get me and Danny back together."

Clara's mouth dropped open. A moment later, she shut it and then shook her head. "Say that again? I thought I heard you say that Danny's date is in town to play Cupid for you and your ex."

The word *Cupid* made Marissa's stomach turn. She pressed a hand to her abdomen and said, "Not Cupid. She's a sugar plum fairy."

"You're kidding, right?" Clara grinned as she completely abandoned her cookies and reached for the nog. "You have a sugar plum fairy? That's amazing. And her mission is to bring you and Danny back together? Oh. Em. Gee. You're living your own holiday movie, Marissa!"

"This is not a movie, Clara!" Marissa took a gulp of her Irish cream coffee and shook her head. "It's... it's..." She didn't know what it was, but it wasn't a movie.

"Romantic?" Clara's eyes gleamed as she tugged Marissa over to the kitchen table and gestured for her to sit. "This calls for something decadent."

Marissa eyed the batter on the counter and wondered if they were going to have to wait until they were baked.

But Clara suddenly produced a plate of double chocolate fudge cookies and brought them to the table. Once she had one in hand, she said, "Okay. Now I'm ready. Tell me everything."

"According to the sugar plum fairy, Danny was cursed," Marissa said and then launched into the entire story. She told her about Sophie's sister being in love with Danny and enacting her revenge. And how Danny hadn't known and had followed her advice, which led to their destruction. "Now she says we can break the curse if we spend a lot more time together and learn to trust each other again."

Clara pressed her hand to her heart, looking wounded. "Marissa, what are you doing here? Shouldn't you be with Danny?"

"Why would I do that? He left me. You do understand

that he made the decision to leave without even telling me why, right?"

"Sure, but he did it for a good reason." Clara let out a sigh, looking like she'd just read her favorite romance novel. "You have to admit, it was really selfless of him to leave to keep you safe."

"No, I don't have to admit any such thing." Marissa picked up a cookie and broke it in half. But then instead of eating it, she put it on a napkin, deciding she wasn't hungry. "Don't you understand? He decided our lives for us back then. He didn't respect me enough to include me in what was going on. I was destroyed. Danny was my entire world. And now, I've made a good life for myself. I don't need to rely on him or anyone else. Just because he's inserted himself back into my life, it doesn't mean I need to go running back to him."

"You don't trust him," Clara said with a small nod.

"It's not that. I..." Marissa trailed off. She had been going to say that marriage just wasn't for her. That she'd been too young to know her own mind back then. But the fact was her friend had hit the nail on the head. "You're right. I don't."

She smiled softly. "But you still love him."

"No I don't," she said automatically.

"You do. I can see it in your eyes." Clara got up out of her chair and then wrapped her arms around Marissa's neck as she gave her a hug and a kiss on the cheek. "I know it's scary, but our hearts don't lie. How could you not love him?"

Marissa wiped away one lone tear as she shook her

head. "I will always love Danny Frost. But I can't get involved with him again. It took me way too long to recover when he left."

"You're scared he'll leave again," Clara whispered. "But for what it's worth, Mar, I think you are both different people now. Since your relationship was torn apart by a curse, I think you both owe it to yourselves to find out if there's still a spark there."

Marissa shook her head. "That's because you're a true romantic. The Romeo and Juliet type of romantic. I'm not. He hurt me once. I'm not interested in letting it happen again."

Clara tightened her hold, squeezing Marissa one last time before she straightened and nodded. "That's understandable." She went into her kitchen and stuffed the batter in the refrigerator. "We need to get some fresh air. Want to take Pumpkin on a walk?"

"That's a good idea." Marissa went next door to her house, changed her clothes, and then got her sweet girl dressed in her harness vest. After grabbing her leash and a couple of pickup bags, the pair went out front to meet Clara.

Her friend was dressed in yoga pants, a sweatshirt, and tennis shoes. The outfit was very similar to Marissa's, although she was wearing leggings and an oversized T-shirt. Even though it'd been snowing out, Marissa welcomed the cold if it would numb her anger and frustration.

"You're going to freeze," Clara said, eyeing her bare arms.

"I'll be fine. I have enough rage to fuel the entire west end."

Clara just shook her head and reached down to pick up Pumpkin and give her a kiss. The dog's tail was working overtime from excitement. "Okay, cutie. Let's get our walk on."

The three of them took off down the street, with Marissa still seething about Sophie and Danny just assuming she'd play along with some sort of reconciliation. She was a grown woman who hadn't been waiting around her entire adult life for some man to walk back into it. He was going to have to do a heck of a lot better than that if he wanted any relationship with her, much less a romantic one.

"You're vibrating," Clara said, eyeing her.

"I am not," Marissa said.

"Yes you are. You need a massage. Or a beer."

"How about both?" Marissa pulled out her phone. "We should have a spa day. Now."

"That would be great if they weren't already closed," Clara said, holding her phone up to show it was after five.

"Ugh. Fine. A beer it is." She was just putting her phone back in her pocket when it rang. She frowned when Danny's name flashed on the screen. She scowled, irritated that she hadn't deleted his contact information years ago. Her frustration had reached a boiling point, and she hit the Accept button. "You shouldn't be calling me, Danny. I said I needed—"

"Marissa, thank the gods," Danny said. "Listen—"

"No, you listen, I told—"

"Marissa! You and Clara need to get off the sidewalk right now. A car is headed straight for you!"

She glanced up just in time to see a white SUV jump the curb on the opposite side of the road and immediately spin out of control in their direction. Crying out, Marissa grabbed Clara by the hand and yanked her and Pumpkin into the yard. Both of them stumbled and fell, landing in a heap while the white SUV jumped the sidewalk where they'd just been walking and took out a mailbox as it came to a stop.

"Pumpkin!" Marissa cried, looking for her dog.

Her sweet pup popped up right next to her, shaking as she leaned against Marissa's body.

"Thank the goddesses." Marissa wrapped her arm around her baby and gave her kisses, soothing her.

"Marissa?" a faint voice called from her phone. She glanced around, looking for it. She must have dropped it somewhere when she face-planted in the yard.

"Danny, is that you?" Clara asked, talking into the phone. Her lips curved into a smile. "Thank you. I think you just saved all three of our butts."

As Clara praised Danny for letting them know about his vision in time for them to get out of the way, Marissa got up off the lawn and tried to brush the grass stains from her leggings. It didn't work.

When Clara ended the call and handed Marissa the phone, she said, "He just saved our lives."

"He does that," Marissa said.

"What if he can't call the next time he has a vision? Or you don't pick up?"

"I'll pick up," she said.

"Even if you don't hear it at the bar?" Clara asked.

"I mean… I'll do my best," Marissa promised, hating that she'd dragged her best friend into her drama.

"Wouldn't it just be easier to break the curse? Find a way to forgive him? Otherwise, I think your luck can only go so far. One of these days you will get hurt, and then what? You'll have your pride and independence, but who knows what shape you'll be in? Who will watch Pumpkin while you heal?"

"You!" Marissa was so tired, and she didn't want to have this conversation.

"Of course, right. I just don't want the accident to happen at all," Clara said.

Marissa looked at her shaken friend and nodded slowly. That *had* been a close call. If no one had been with her, maybe Marissa could continue to act as if the curse wasn't a big deal. But if it endangered other people she cared about, ignoring it wasn't an option.

There was only one solution. Work with Danny until the craziness settled down. And in the meantime, find some way to trust the one man she'd resented for over a decade.

CHAPTER 12

*D*anny stared at the phone, unable to shake the uneasy feeling in his gut. He'd been throwing mugs on the wheel when the vision of a car hitting Marissa and Clara had hit him with an intensity he hadn't felt since he and Marissa had still been together.

He'd been lucky that her number was still the same. If she hadn't picked up... He shuddered thinking about the consequences. The last time he'd been this shaken, he'd thought the only way to keep Marissa safe was to run away. But Sophie had said that in order to break the curse, they needed to spend time together and learn to trust each other.

He wondered what he would have done back then if he'd known he'd been cursed. He definitely would have tried harder before he'd bolted.

Now that they were in the same town again, it was clear that their proximity had re-triggered the curse. He could either run away again or find a way to repair their relationship. This time he wasn't running. He had a successful business, and he'd reconnected with his cousins, giving him the family he craved after his grandmother passed. Plus, if there was any chance to have Marissa back in his life, he was going to take it.

She'd been his best friend before he'd fallen in love with her. After he left her, his life hadn't ever been the same again.

He rubbed at a spot over his heart. The dull ache almost never went away, only now it appeared to be intensifying. It was like a scab had been ripped off and he now had an open wound.

In his mind, there was only one thing to do. They needed to spend time together. But what was he going to do? Just show up at her house? He didn't even know where she lived. Though he supposed that wouldn't be hard to figure out. It wasn't as if Christmas Grove was that big a town.

He sat at his wheel, finished the mug he'd been making when the vision hit, and then went about the business of cleaning up his shop for the night. Just when he was ready to turn out the lights, there was a soft knock on the back door.

Frowning, he opened the door and then raised his eyebrows in surprise when he found Marissa standing there in her grass-stained leggings and an oversized T-shirt. He studied her carefully, suddenly worried that she'd been hurt dodging the car that had almost hit her. "Marissa, is everything all right?"

She nodded and swept into the studio.

He closed the door and turned to watch her.

Marissa wrung her hands as she glanced around, clearly nervous. "I, um, want to thank you for the help today. The phone call, I mean."

"You don't need to thank me for anything. All I did was make a phone call," he said, unsure why his nerves were buzzing. He'd been terrified when the vision had hit him, but by the time he got off the phone with Clara, he'd known Marissa was all right. And while the whole curse thing was unsettling, he had managed to calm down while finishing his last mug. But seeing her there, looking vulnerable, made him want to scoop her up in his arms and keep her safe forever.

"Yes I do," she said, meeting his eyes. Her expression was full of nervous energy. "I owe you an apology, too. This afternoon, I didn't take the news well and…"

There was silence as Danny waited for her to finish her thought. When she didn't, he said, "And?"

Marissa blew out a breath and he knew that she was finally going to finish her thought. "I think we need to take Sophie's advice to heart."

"Okay." What did that mean exactly? "Are you saying you want to spend more time together?"

Her lips curved down as she grimaced, but she nodded. "Clara is worried about me."

"So am I," he said honestly.

"She's afraid that you'll have a vision and not be able to get in touch with me."

"I've had that same thought," Danny admitted. "But what do we do about that?"

She hesitated and then suddenly blurted, "We have to break the curse."

He'd thought that was fairly obvious. "The only way to do that is—"

"We need to move in together."

Her words hung between them in the deafening silence. Had Danny heard her right? Had she really just suggested that they move in together after being apart for sixteen years? Although it was exactly what he wanted, he also couldn't ignore the unease that had formed in his gut.

"I mean, we should share a house. Get to know each other again. Just long enough to break the curse and then we can get on with our lives. Sophie said we needed to spend time together. Figure out how to trust one another again, right? Well, let's do that. Pumpkin almost became an orphan today, and I'm nowhere near ready to give up my place on this earth. So, what do you say?"

"Pumpkin?" he asked, the name triggering something in his memory that he couldn't quite place.

"My dog. I was walking her when that car came right for us."

The image of a sable-colored dog flashed in his mind, and suddenly he remembered the dream he'd had with the two of them sitting on their porch. The dog's name had been Pumpkin. A lump formed in his throat as he wondered if that had been some sort of premonition. It couldn't be, could it? He'd never had a vision in a dream before. But the name had been right.

Maybe he'd just overheard someone talking about her dog Pumpkin and had incorporated her into his dream. It was possible that Jackson had said something about her.

"Danny?" Marissa asked, breaking into his thoughts.

He swallowed the lump and cleared his throat. "I live in a one-bedroom apartment. So I'm afraid my place would be a tight squeeze."

She let out a sigh of relief. "That's okay. I have a two bedroom. We could just be roommates while we get to know each other again."

"I also have a cat. Bells. She's just one year old, so really still a kitten. She'd have to come with me," he said. Bells was a dealbreaker. He was already concerned that he left her alone too much while he was working.

Marissa smiled softly. "You have a cat? You always wanted one."

He nodded. They'd talked about getting a kitten right after they were married, but both of them had school and work, and neither were home often. They'd decided it wasn't fair to bring in a pet when they rarely had time for each other, let alone a pet that was dependent on them for everything. "She sort of just popped into my life last year and instantly stole my heart."

"That's sweet. Bells is welcome. Pumpkin likes other animals, so as long as Bells isn't afraid of her, I'm sure they'll get along fine."

Danny stared at her, more than a little stunned at this turn of events. But then he nodded. "Okay. Are you sure, though?"

Her eyes hardened with determination as she said, "I'm

sure. I don't want to be crushed by falling things or run down on the sidewalk all because of some crazy fairy who cursed us years before. It's time to fix this so that we can all just move on with our lives. If the fastest way to do that is to spend time together and heal what's transpired between us, then I think that's what we should do. We're not kids anymore, Danny. It's time to be grownups and put this all behind us."

He certainly agreed with her about fixing the situation, but Danny felt sure that when it came to Marissa, he was never going to be able to move on. But still he nodded and said, "I'll need to go home, pack some clothes, and get Bells. Do you want me to pick up dinner on the way back to your place?"

She shook her head. "No. I've already got something laid out for dinner. I'll make enough for both of us." She reached into her bag and pulled out a key. "This is for you. I'll text you the address."

"Thanks," he said as relief rushed through him. The feeling was quickly followed by a trickle of anxiety. What if Sophie's solution didn't work? Would their arrangement only make things worse? He quickly shook his head. There was no point in inviting trouble.

"Okay. I'll see you later tonight then," Marissa said and walked out.

Danny watched her go and then finished locking up. As he started his 4Runner, a hint of a smile claimed his lips. For the first time in sixteen years, he was going home to the only woman he'd ever loved.

CHAPTER 13

*M*arissa tucked in the fresh sheet on the guest bed and wondered if she'd lost her mind. Would she wake up the next morning and find out that this day had all been some sort of crazy nightmare? Would she learn that there were no such things as sugar plum fairies? And would she be disappointed when she realized that Danny wasn't in her guest room?

How was it possible she'd woken up that morning thinking that she'd get her chocolate chip pancakes at Candy Canes and then spend the rest of the afternoon decorating and drinking nog with her girlfriends. Instead, she'd done both of those things and then gotten into a clay fight with a sugar plum fairy, nearly got herself run down by a car, and then invited Danny to live with her.

She sat down heavily on the bed and buried her head in her hands. It had been a long-ass day and all she wanted to do was sink into a hot bath with a bottle of wine and pretend that none of this had happened.

Instead, she stood, finished making the bed, and then got out a dust rag and started wiping down her baseboards. If Danny was moving in, she couldn't have him thinking that she'd been slacking on her deep cleaning.

Once the baseboards were gleaming, she walked into the guest bathroom and got to work. The room was rarely used, so after a brief spruce, everything was sparkling.

Marissa walked out into the living room and then reached for the duster, intending to dust the ceiling fan. But when Pumpkin barked and gave her a look of judgment, she put the duster back into the closet and sat heavily in her oversized chair. "I know. I'm going overboard."

Her pup jumped up into her lap and licked her face.

"Thanks, girl. I needed that." Marissa scratched her dog behind the ears and then laughed when Pumpkin flopped down on her lap and rolled over, putting her paws in the air. There wasn't much more in life that Pumpkin loved more than her belly rubs. "I hope you don't mind a little bit of company. Danny and his kitty, Bells, are coming to stay with us for a bit."

Pumpkin's tongue was hanging out as she reveled in the attention.

"I know you don't care right now. Not when you're getting everything you ever wanted, but I'm going to need you to be nice to Bells. Understand?"

Pumpkin turned her head and looked right at Marissa. She blinked once and then let her head roll back again.

Marissa laughed. "I knew I could count on you."

There was a knock on the door, and Pumpkin immediately rolled over and jumped off her mistress's lap, barking incessantly at the door.

"It's just Danny and Bells, Pumpkin. You don't need to bark," Marissa said as she opened the door.

Pumpkin's barking intensified, even as her tail started to wag with vigor.

Danny stared down at her, his eyes wide with surprise.

"She's just excited," Marissa quickly reassured him.

"I see that," he said, still staring at the dog. When he looked up, he said, "She's beautiful. How long have you had her?"

"About five years. I got her not long after I opened the pub." Marissa scooped Pumpkin up and held her close to her chest. "She's a sweetie."

"I can tell." They stood there awkwardly for a few beats until Marissa let out a nervous chuckle. "Sorry. Come on in."

"Thanks." He hefted a large duffel bag onto his shoulder and then picked up the hard-sided pet carrier that was near his feet.

"Your room is this way," Marissa said as she set Pumpkin on the floor and took a deep breath, trying to calm her rapidly beating heart. She'd known it would be strange to have Danny at her house, but she hadn't anticipated just how much she'd wanted him there. When they reached his room, she pushed the door open and took a step back. "This one is yours. Mine is across the hall."

He walked in and placed his bag on the bed. Then he knelt down and opened the carrier. The cutest black and white cat poked her head out and meowed.

Pumpkin darted into the room, but slowed just before she got to the cat and then lowered her head as if she were saying hi.

The two bumped noses and then Bells walked completely out of the carrier and rubbed her body on Pumpkin's legs. It didn't take long until Pumpkin turned and ran out of the room with Bells following quickly behind her.

"I guess they're fast friends," Danny said, giving Marissa an easy smile.

"Looks like it." She cleared her throat. "The bathroom across the hall is yours. Feel free to set up Bells's litter box in there. I'll go finish getting dinner together while you get settled."

"Thanks, Marissa," he said, his green eyes holding hers.

"I should be thanking you. I'm not the one who had to leave my home." She gave him a grateful smile and quickly disappeared into the kitchen. After pulling the lasagna out of the oven, she grabbed plates and watched as Pumpkin playfully chased Bells around the dining room. When Bells stopped and hid partially behind one of the table legs, Pumpkin waited patiently while her tail went a hundred miles an hour. There was no question that Pumpkin was happy to have a playmate. Bells seemed a little more cautious, but when Pumpkin let out a bark and then darted into the living room, Bells took off after her, and Marissa knew they'd get along just fine.

Marissa was setting the table when she heard the front door open and then close.

A couple of minutes later, Danny appeared, holding a bottle of wine. "Do you still like pinot grigio?"

"You brought me pinot?" Marissa asked as a smile claimed her lips.

"Yes. Is it still your wine of choice?"

Laughing, she nodded. "I can't believe you remember that." It wasn't as if they'd spent a lot of time drinking wine. After all, they had only been nineteen when they'd separated. Though her dad had let her drink wine at dinner, and the crisp white pinot grigio had been her absolute favorite.

"Of course I remember." He stepped into the kitchen and started opening drawers until he found the corkscrew.

It amazed Marissa that she didn't find him invasive. If that had been anyone else besides Clara or Felicity, she'd have been annoyed enough to ban them from her kitchen. Especially while she was still getting dinner together. But Danny... He just felt right in her space.

Marissa placed their dinner on the table and said, "I assume you still like lasagna?"

"Who doesn't like lasagna?" he asked as he poured each of them a glass of wine.

"People who are low carb?" she guessed, taking the glass he offered her.

"Sucks to be them." He winked and then sat across

from her. He picked up the serving spoon and gestured to her plate.

She held her plate up for him, letting him serve. Once they both had plates full of pasta, Marissa held her wine glass up. "To new beginnings."

Something unreadable flashed in his eyes just before he touched his glass to hers and repeated her toast. Their eyes met and held as they each took a sip.

A bark came from the other room, followed closely by the sound of something crashing to the floor. Marissa jumped up and ran to the living room, finding a picture frame on the floor, the glass broken. Pumpkin and Bells were both sitting there, staring at her as if to say, "It wasn't us!"

She shook her head and chuckled to herself. "I can see you two are going to be trouble with a capital T, aren't you?"

Both just stared at her with innocent expressions on their faces.

"Looks like we're in trouble with those two," Danny said from behind her.

She turned around and raised one eyebrow. "Your cat is a bad influence on my dog."

"No doubt." He walked back into the kitchen and returned a moment later with her broom and dustpan in hand.

"You don't have to do that," she said, reaching for the broom.

But Danny pulled them away from her and shook his

head. "This wouldn't have happened if Bells and I hadn't moved in. It's only right that I take care of it."

Marissa shook her head at him but couldn't help feeling pleased. It felt like old times when it had just been them in their little apartment. He'd always done small things for her while she'd cooked for him. At least that's the way it had been in the beginning. As their lives got busier and busier with school and work, their nights together had been few and far between, but there had been a time when they'd spent many nights just like this.

"All set," Danny said after he was finished cleaning up. "I put the picture of you and Pumpkin back on the table. The frame didn't make it, I'm afraid."

"Thank you," she said, topping off both of the glasses of wine. "I'll get a new one after Christmas when everything is on sale."

"Sounds like a plan." He picked up his fork and dug into his lasagna.

Marissa watched as his eyes rolled to the back of his head and he let out a moan of pleasure. Heat coiled in her belly, and suddenly she wasn't hungry at all. Instead, she wanted to walk over, sit in his lap, and bury her hands in his hair as she kissed him senseless.

The vision of her fantasy was so strong she nearly acted on it, but when she heard the scrape of the chair on her hardwood floor, she snapped out of it and forced herself to stay seated and take a bite of her lasagna.

"So tell me how you ended up here in Christmas Grove, owning a pottery shop," she said.

"Only if you tell me how you ended up owning a pub," he countered.

She grinned at him. "Deal."

"Okay, here goes." He took a gulp of his wine and then said, "After I left, you already know that I transferred schools."

Her heart ached, but she did her best to refrain from showing any emotion. That was all in the past, and she didn't want to rehash all the pain they'd both suffered back then. She knew now that Danny hadn't wanted to leave, and that he'd only done it to protect her. And while intellectually, she understood, she was still very hurt that he hadn't trusted her enough to tell her why. "Yeah. I knew that."

"After graduation, I went to work for an accounting firm. It was pretty much everything you can imagine. Dull. Predictable. Stressful during end of year. The firm was fine, but I hated working for someone else. Eventually, I started my own practice. It was a decent living. I liked working for myself, but I never was passionate about numbers."

"And pottery? Did you do that in your spare time? As a hobby?" she asked, fascinated. When they were together, he'd always been the one who was worried about security. How they were going to set themselves up for their future. She'd been the one who'd always talked about what it would be like if they followed a different path. One that didn't look like everyone else they knew.

"Actually yes." His cheeks turned pink as he glanced away. But when he looked at her again, he continued.

"Once I started my own firm and was able to set my own hours, I started taking pottery classes. Before long, I had a small pottery setup in my garage, and I started selling my mugs at craft fairs once a month. It was really cool to have people actually want to buy my stuff."

"So one day you decided to chuck the practice and move here of all places?" she asked, knowing she sounded a little bit accusatory.

He laughed. "No. Actually, I was here last Christmas with my grandmother, my parents, and my cousins Atlas and Alison. It was my grandmother's wish that we were all together one last time. She passed after Christmas, and that's when I decided to reevaluate my life choices. I didn't want to spend my entire life doing something I didn't love." He paused and stared at her. "I think that's something you can relate to."

"Yes," she said softly. "It is."

He nodded. "I figured that hadn't changed. Anyway, since Zach and Atlas are here and it's the last place where I spent time with my grandmother, it just seemed like the perfect place to open my shop. I honestly had no idea you were here. But I can't say I'm sorry to see you again."

"Oh." Marissa wasn't sure what to say. Instead, she picked up their empty plates and started to clear the table.

"I didn't say that to make you uncomfortable, Marissa. I was just... being honest," he said.

"I know." She loaded the plates into the dishwasher. Then she said, "I wasn't happy to see you at all."

He let out a bark of laughter. "I gathered that."

"But now..." She shrugged and walked back over to the

table, taking her seat. "I suppose finding out the truth of what happened back then is good closure for me. And once this curse is broken, maybe we can both find some peace."

His expression turned blank before he blinked and nodded. "Yes, closure would be better than the way we left things back then."

She got the feeling that wasn't at all what he wanted to say, but he held his tongue, and for that she was grateful. Whatever he was thinking, she wasn't ready to hear it. Not now. Not when she was still conflicted about how everything had gone down.

"So you ended up here. Are you happy with your move?" she asked, genuinely curious.

"Very. I wish I'd done it years earlier. It was hard getting up and running, but business is good, and I love being near family. Plus, Christmas Grove has stolen a little piece of my heart. I can't think of anywhere I'd rather be."

Marissa let out a small sigh and smiled. "I feel the same way. You know this town has always been special to me."

Danny nodded. "I do."

"My dad passed away six years ago. After that, I just had to get out of his house. Had to move somewhere that didn't hold a bunch of sad memories. Christmas Grove has always held magic for me, so I sold Dad's house, bought this place, and opened Sleighed. I've never looked back. It might be the best decision I ever made. I now have my two best friends that live next door and Pumpkin. All three of them make my life better. Plus, there's Jackson and Kira, who work with me, and they're like family, too. What's not to love?"

"Your two best friends live next door? Clara and Felicity?" he asked.

"Yep. It's Clara's house, and Felicity rents a room from her. Both can afford to live on their own, but they like the company. I like that they are right next door. We have our weekly rituals. Sundays at Candy Canes and usually we have Wednesday night drinks."

He nodded, looking pleased for her. "You've built a really nice life for yourself, Marissa. I hope it's not condescending to say that I'm proud of you."

She thought about it for a moment. If he'd said that at any other time before she'd invited him to stay with her while they worked on neutralizing the curse, she'd have been offended. But now that they were building a tentative friendship, all she felt was pride. "No, it's not. Thank you."

"No need to thank me. You did this all on your own. It's really impressive. Sleighed is the town watering hole. A place that would be really missed if it wasn't there. You've built something special for the people of Christmas Grove."

Her face heated, and she knew she was blushing when she said, "I really hope so."

He reached out and squeezed her hand. "You have."

She stared at their connection for a long moment before pulling her hand back and standing. "It's late. I need to finish cleaning up and take Pumpkin out before I go to bed."

"You take care of Pumpkin. I'll clean up," he said, already reaching for the dish in the middle of the table.

"You don't have to do that," Marissa said. "I can—"

"You cooked," he said as he took the dish to the kitchen. "It's the least I can do."

She watched as he rummaged around and found the lid to the glass pan. As he was putting it in the fridge, she gave up the fight and said, "Okay. Thanks."

A moment later, she found her dog curled up with his cat in her oversize chair. Chuckling to herself, she gently lifted her dog, trying not to disturb the cat. Pumpkin groaned like an eighty-year-old, making her chuckle. "Come on, girl. Time to go out before we hit the sack."

Pumpkin blinked up at her with sleepy eyes, and Marissa felt the tiniest bit guilty for disturbing her. But twenty minutes later, when they were curled up together in Marissa's bed, Pumpkin's head on her chest, she whispered, "Love you, baby girl."

Pumpkin gave her a kiss on her hand and started snoring softly.

This is all I need, Marissa thought. *My pup and a warm bed.*

But then why was it that all she could think about was the man who was in the next room?

CHAPTER 14

"*H*ere you go, cutie," Danny said as he handed Pumpkin a treat. Pumpkin gingerly took the treat from him, and as soon as she had a decent grip on it, she ran full speed to her dog bed in the living room. Bells sat at Danny's feet, watching the overly excited pup. When she disappeared, Bells looked up at Danny and yawned.

He chuckled. "She does have a lot of energy. I bet she wears you out."

The cat rubbed against his leg until he reached down and scooped her up. She snuggled into his chest, content as he scratched her ears.

It was Wednesday, three days after he'd moved into Marissa's house, and although they hadn't seen much of each other, so far, he'd only had two visions of her, both of them minor. One had been of a glass falling at the pub that resulted in a minor cut, and the other had been a flat tire that could have caused her to be stranded on the side of the road. But because he'd warned her, she'd been able to avoid both accidents. He couldn't be sure, but it seemed likely that because they were sharing a house and spent more time in proximity to another, that the curse had lessened in intensity. At least he hoped that was what was going on. Maybe if they at least managed to repair their friendship, it would be enough to break the curse entirely.

He certainly hoped so. Because while he'd love to pick up where they left off sixteen years ago, it was clear to him that they were different people now, with different goals and priorities. There couldn't be any move toward any sort of romantic relationship until they got to know each other better.

Unfortunately, he hadn't seen as much of her as he'd hoped. With Marissa working in the evenings and him working during the day, unless he went to the pub or stayed up late, he was unlikely to see her at all. However, she had taken to leaving him dinner in the fridge and he'd reciprocated by making sure she had coffee ready in the pot before she got up.

It was a nice setup, but unless he was willing to stalk her at the pub every night, his only interaction had been through notes that they left each other on the counter.

He glanced at the clock. It was just after five. He'd left work early so that he'd have time to stop in at Marissa's to clean up before heading over to Zach's tree farm. It was the annual Christmas Tree Festival that night. Zach had generously offered him a table to sell his pottery, so Danny had spent a few days the week before making special mugs for the occasion. He wasn't sure what to expect, but either way, he was happy to be included.

Before he headed to the shower, he opened the refrigerator door and was disappointed to see that Marissa hadn't left him dinner. Not that she was obligated to feed him. He just liked knowing that she'd thought of him. He shut the door and grabbed a cookie from the jar, telling himself he'd pick up something on the way to Zach's.

"Pumpkin just scammed you," Marissa said, walking into the kitchen. "That's her third treat in the last hour."

He jerked his head up in surprise. "Marissa, I didn't even know you were here."

"It's my day off." She smirked at him. "I do take days off, you know."

"I should hope so," he said with a smile. "I didn't see your car outside."

"It's still at the shop. They're doing the alignment and rotating tires while they fix the flat. I should have it back tomorrow." She walked into the kitchen, paused to scratch Bells's ears and then headed for the fridge. "Are you hungry? I was just about to make something to eat."

He wanted to say yes. Wanted to sit down and have dinner with her like he had on Sunday. But he didn't have time. "I'd love to, but I've got to get a quick shower and head out to the Christmas Tree Festival."

"Oh, right. That's tonight," Marissa said, looking thoughtful. "Are you participating in the craft booths or just helping Zach?"

"I have a table." He finished off his cookie. "You should

come by if you're not working... Wait, you don't have a car. You could ride with me if you don't mind staying the entire time."

Her eyes lit up, and he was sure she was about to say yes, but then she gave him a slight frown. "I would, but it's girls' night. Clara and Felicity are coming over. It's sort of a ritual. Tonight we're supposed to make our annual holiday cookies for our staff holiday parties."

"That sounds like fun, too," he said, though his response lacked enthusiasm. He was surprised at how disappointed he was. The invite had been a spur of the moment thing. And he'd be busy working his booth.

"It always is," she said, though she didn't sound any more enthusiastic than he did.

"I'd better get cleaned up." Danny hurried past her to his bathroom and took a quick shower. Fifteen minutes later, he walked back into the kitchen and was surprised when she handed him a brown paper bag. "What's this?"

"I made you a roast beef sandwich. I hope you still like cheddar cheese. I left off the onions since you'll be dealing with the public," she said with a wink. "There's this also." She handed him a thermos. "Hot coffee to keep you warm."

He held the bag and the thermos, warmth spreading through him. The urge to lean down and kiss her overtook him, but he took a small step back, trying to keep from falling under her spell. "Thank you, Marissa. This is really thoughtful."

She shrugged. "I'd do it for any of my friends."

"Friends?" he repeated as he smiled down at her. "Is that what we are?"

She flushed slightly but didn't look away. "We're sharing a house and looking after each other. I'd say it's a good start, wouldn't you?"

"Yes." Danny nodded, and then deciding to throw caution to the wind, he moved forward and brushed his lips over her cheek as he whispered, "You're the best."

The flush deepened on her cheeks, and he couldn't help but be pleased with himself.

"Go. Before you're late. And good luck. I hope you sell out." She waved him off.

Danny just stood there, taking in her fresh appearance. She was barefoot, wearing jeans and a red Christmas sweater, and she'd pulled her red hair into a sleek ponytail. He wanted to put the food down, call his cousin and tell him he couldn't make it, and then curl up on the couch with her while they cuddled and watched heartwarming holiday flicks. It was something she'd always wanted to do when they were younger, but he'd always argued, insisting that they watch something they'd both enjoy, like *Die Hard* or *Home Alone*. He'd been such a dumb kid back then. Because tonight, he'd gladly put on any holiday movie she wanted just so he could be near her.

"Danny?" she said. "Something wrong?"

"Huh? Oh, no." He scrambled for something to say that wouldn't out him as a lovesick sap who wanted nothing more than to watch cheesy holiday movies with his ex. "I was just thinking that I could use a baking night sometime this week, too. It would be nice to offer some cookies to the customers as they come in to do their Christmas shopping."

"I can leave some recipes out for you if you'd like," she offered.

"That would be great." He thanked her again for the food and then hurried out of the house before he did something stupid, like confess that he'd never stopped loving her. Once he was in his 4Runner, he let out a long sigh and hoped he'd get home in time to watch one of those holiday movies after all.

"THERE YOU ARE!" Zach said when Danny finally walked through the gates of the Frost Family Tree Farm. The place was buzzing with activity. Other artists were busy setting up their booths. They had everything from handmade soaps to original paintings. Although he was surprised to find Clara there with her blown glass after Marissa had indicated they were having girls' night.

He left his handcart at his table and walked over to her booth. She had two tables full of different snow globes. Each depicted a magical snowy scene from Christmas Grove. And to his surprise, he saw one that actually had his shop inside. He immediately picked it up and admired the detail. In addition to his store sign, Pottery Grove, there were also very small pots and mugs in the windows of his gallery.

"Clara, this is amazing. Did you do all this work yourself?" he asked her.

The bubbly dark-haired beauty spun around, noticing him for the first time. "I did! Please tell me I got the details right. It's always a little stressful when I use a real place in these. I wouldn't want to spell something wrong or, goddess forbid, add a cat when there's supposed to be a dog."

The slightly nervous energy coming off her just added to her charm and made Danny smile as he said, "It's perfect. In fact, it's so spot on that I want to buy it. Do you take credit cards?"

"Of course," she said, beaming as she pulled it from his hands. "But for you, it's half price."

"You don't have to do that," he said, shaking his head as he frowned at her. As a craftsperson himself, he knew just how easy it was to be tempted to give away his work when someone was excited about it. It was something he suspected he'd always battle. But he'd be damned if he let a fellow artist shortchange themselves, especially when there was no reason to. "It's worth more than double what your regular price is anyway."

"But you fixed my kiln. For free, I might add. And if you hadn't done that, this table wouldn't be full tonight." She wrapped the globe up in brown paper and placed it into a holiday themed paper bag. As she handed it to him, she added, "Don't argue with me, or I won't charge you anything at all."

He let out a bark of laughter and shook his head. "Fine. You win. But only this one time. After this, we're even."

She just smirked at him. "We'll see."

Danny opened his mouth to tell her that she was impossible, but his eyesight blurred and a vision hit him, sending horror through his entire body. The moment he came out of the trance, he leaped into action, running full out toward the large Christmas tree in the middle of the clearing. Just before he reached his destination, a large man threw a punch, knocking a taller thinner man right into the tree.

Danny saw the mother's eyes of the small child widen in horror as she lurched for her son just as the tree started to topple. He jumped in front of them, his arms wide, taking the full brunt of the tree as it fell right on him. He landed sideways, flat on his back, the wind knocked out of him and the tree pinning him down.

There were screams and cries all around him, but Danny couldn't see anything except Christmas tree needles.

"Danny!" Zach called. "Danny, are you okay?"

"Is the kid okay?" Danny huffed out.

"The kid? What kid?" Zach asked, moving a branch so that Danny could see his face.

"The toddler. The one that was standing here a second ago." Everything hurt, though not enough for Danny to think there was any permanent damage.

"He's fine," a woman's voice said right before the petite blonde appeared in his field of vision. "You saved him. Thank you. Thank you. Thank you."

Danny closed his eyes and let out a sigh of relief. "Good. As long as he's safe."

"Don't pass out on me," Zach said. "We're going to get this tree off you in just a moment. But don't move. Not until the paramedic gets a look at you, got it?"

"Sure," Danny said, blinking to try to keep his eyes open. The lights were causing his head to throb.

It wasn't long before the tree was removed from Danny's body. He lay there in the dirt, staring up at the crowd gathering around him. He blinked, his vision starting to clear now that the lights from the tree weren't blinding him.

"How are you doing, Danny?" a woman with a small flashlight asked as she pointed the light right into one eye.

He winced and tried to look away. "I was better before you blinded me with that light."

She chuckled softly. "Feisty. That's a good sign."

Danny frowned at her. "Can I get up now? This ground is cold."

"I bet. Let me just check you out a little bit first."

"Nothing is broken," he complained.

But she *tsked* and told him she'd be the judge of that. After thoroughly inspecting his limbs and shining the light into his eyes one more time, she sat back. "Okay. I think you'll live. I don't see any signs of broken bones or a concussion. But you'll probably be a little bruised for a few days. If you need anything for the pain, head to the urgent care. Got it?"

"Sure, doc." He gingerly sat up and winced when his back complained.

Zach held out a hand, helping him to his feet. He was wet and dirty from the melted snow, but other than shuffling like an old man due to his back, he decided he hadn't suffered any permanent damage.

"What happened to the two bozos who decided to pummel each other's faces?" Danny asked Zach as he sat down in his chair at his table.

"Idiots. They've been hauled off to the drunk tank at the sheriff's office. Turns out they'd had a little too much cheer before they came here and decided to have a fist fight over a girl they were both trying to date. Neither of them are worth talking about. However, the fact that you saved that kid? Now *that* is going to be the town news for the next few days. I hope you're ready to be the local hero."

Danny groaned. "I don't need all that. I was just trying to—"

"There you are!" the petite blonde cried as she hurried over. Her son was in her arms and wrapped around her body, holding on for dear life. "What can I do to repay you?"

"Repay me?" Danny asked. "There's nothing to repay me for. I'm just glad no one was hurt."

"I just don't know what I would have done if you hadn't saved Benji. That tree could have crushed him." There were tears in her eyes as her voice trembled. "You're a hero, Danny Frost."

"I'm not, but that's kind," he said.

"You are. Just you wait and see." Then she glanced down at the mugs he'd placed on the table. "Did you make these?"

"I did," he said.

"I'll take four."

"You don't have—" he started.

The woman handed him her credit card. "Go ahead and charge me. I'm going to get Benji settled in his car seat and send my husband back to pick those up."

Danny stared after her for a second, still holding her credit card.

Zach chuckled. "Get used to hearing that tonight. I bet you sell out within the hour."

As his cousin walked off, Danny sat back in his chair and desperately wished once again that he was back at Marissa's, watching one of those holiday movies instead of starring in his own Christmas disaster flick.

CHAPTER 15

"*W*here's Clara?" Marissa asked as Felicity strode into her kitchen looking like she was dressed for an office holiday party. She had on red wool pants, a green formfitting sweater, and had her long blond hair in a fancy bun tied up with a red ribbon. "And where have you been? That doesn't look like cookie baking attire."

Felicity frowned at her. "Clara is at the Christmas Tree Festival. Where else would she be?"

Marissa jerked her head up from her cookie batter. "I thought she declined that invite on account of not having enough inventory."

"She didn't tell you? After Danny fixed her kiln, she got a second wind and made a bunch of snow globes. She's there now. Hopefully killing it. I thought she was going to text you to let you know."

"I don't think she did," Marissa said, patting her pocket

for her phone. When she didn't find it, she hurried over to her charger and found it there with a series of texts from Clara. There was the apology for missing baking night and a promise to make it up to her. "Looks like she did and I was too busy to notice."

"Sounds about right," Felicity said with a laugh. "Should we go over and show her moral support?"

"What about our baking marathon?" Marissa asked, though she was already putting plastic wrap on her bowl, intending to put it in the fridge.

"We'll have to do it Sunday after breakfast."

"Everything always happens after breakfast on Sunday," Marissa said with an amused shake of her head. "Okay, that's fine. Let me just get changed really quickly." If she was going to go out to the festival, she wasn't going to look like Santa's elf with cookie dough smearing her sweater.

Ten minutes later, the pair of them were in the car, headed to the Frost's Christmas tree farm.

"How are things going with Danny?" Felicity asked with a pump of her eyebrows. "Are you two sharing a bed yet?"

Marissa side-eyed her friend. "No. We definitely are not sleeping in the same bed. We barely even know each other now."

"No one said anything about sleeping together. I asked if you were sharing a bed yet. Two entirely different things." Felicity looked at her expectantly as if Marissa was holding back the juicy details.

"Felicity!" Marissa said, shaking her head. "No. There's

nothing going on. But he did kiss me on the cheek tonight when I made him dinner to take to the festival."

"Oh, ho! You made him dinner, did you? That seems a lot more intimate than just sharing a bed for twenty minutes." Felicity was grinning at her.

"You're impossible." Marissa rolled her eyes. "Everything is fine. Nothing is going on between us. We barely even see each other. That's it. The end. Nothing else to report."

"Except that he kissed you on the cheek," she said.

"He was just being nice."

"He was just being a man who wants to get into your pants. But fine. Have it your way. I'm sure he's an angel who only has your best interests at heart." Her tone was sarcastic, but Marissa ignored her.

"I think the curse is fading," Marissa said, eager to get off the topic of what was or wasn't going on between her and Danny. "He's only had two visions, and both were for minor accidents. Nothing like what happened on Sunday."

Felicity sobered, looking serious for the first time that evening. "That's good to hear. I'm not a fan of this curse business. If I had my way, we'd be on a manhunt for that fallen fairy and give her a taste of her own medicine."

It wasn't as if Marissa hadn't thought of that, but if the fairy was powerful enough to saddle them with a curse that could potentially get someone killed, Marissa didn't want to know what else she was capable of. "Let's just work on breaking this curse first. Then maybe something can be done about the rogue sugar plum fairy."

"Fine. But I'm not happy about it," she grumped.

Marissa grinned at her. "I love you."

"I love you, too. Now let's go get our holiday cheer on. I'm in need of something merry."

The parking lot was packed when they arrived at the Frost Family Tree Farm. Instantly Marissa was glad they'd come. There were magical dancing snowmen and candy canes out front under an illusion of falling snow. The line for the hot chocolate was long but moving quickly. And there were small elves running around, handing out cookies to all the kids, keeping them entertained while the adults shopped for arts and crafts, picked out trees, and participated in making their own handmade wreathes from the leftover Christmas tree branches.

They found Clara in her booth, chatting happily with customers. One of her tables was completely bare, and when they asked her how things were going, she gave them two thumbs-up.

Marissa took her time looking through all the craft booths. After picking up a handmade scarf and a bag of homemade soaps, she scanned the area looking for Danny. She knew he was there. She just didn't know where.

Then she spotted him. But he wasn't at a table in the craft section. He was sitting at a long table, helping kids make cranberry and popcorn garland. She walked up and then without thinking about it, she sat right next to him. "Need some help?"

He glanced at her, startled at first, but then a slow smile claimed his lips. "Always. Patty there could use help threading her needle."

Marissa eyed the pretty little redhead and felt an

instant kinship with the little girl. She had a hot chocolate stain on her dress. One of her pigtails had almost come undone, and she had a smudge of dirt on her face. But she was smiling and clearly having the time of her life even as she struggled to get the thread through the needle.

"Here, try this," Marissa said, folding the string in half and showing her how to get the end through the needle.

The girl's eyes lit up and then she started chattering nonstop about everything she'd done at the festival that evening. Marissa barely had a chance to get a word in edgewise, and it wasn't until after the kid's mother collected her that Marissa was able to turn to Danny and ask, "What happened to selling mugs in the craft area?"

"He sold out in the first twenty minutes," Zach said as he strolled up holding an envelope in one hand.

"You did?" Marissa asked as her eyebrows raised. "What did you do, fill those mugs with cold hard cash?"

"Nope. He did something even better. He became the local hero right after we opened." Zach grinned at his cousin.

"Stop," Danny said, rolling his eyes. "All I did was stop a tree from falling on a little boy. Anyone would have done the same."

Marissa smiled softly at Danny, knowing that he'd had a vision and sprang into action. It was one of the reasons she'd fallen in love with him in the first place. He'd always put other people first. Then it dawned on her that the reason that she'd loved him so was the same reason that he'd left her all those years ago, and suddenly she no longer resented him. He was only being the person he'd always been. It was just too bad that it hadn't worked out for them in the end.

But now, who knew what could happen?

Marissa was staring at him, lost in the possibilities of what might be possible if they ever managed to break the curse. She was so out of it that she almost missed Zach's big announcement. She would have if Felicity hadn't nudged her from her other side.

"It's time to reveal this year's Mr. Garland," Zach was saying as he held up the envelope. "In all the years we've been holding this festival, I've never seen this many votes for the same person. It's probably no surprise to anyone that this year's Mr. Garland is none other than Danny Frost!"

Danny blinked up at his cousin. "What?"

"You've won the Mr. Garland prize, cousin. Come on up and get your crown."

Marissa watched as Zach put a crown of garland on Danny's head and the entire crowd gave him a standing ovation.

"You need to lock him down, Mar," Felicity said. "If you don't, someone else will."

Marissa just nodded, because in that moment, all the love she'd ever had for the man standing in front of the crowd came rushing back. She just prayed he wouldn't break her heart again.

CHAPTER 16

"Do you want to watch a movie?" Marissa asked as she stood in the doorway of the kitchen, holding two mugs in her hands. "Or are you too tired after the festival?"

"I'm not too tired," Danny said, even though only a minute ago he'd been considering heading straight to bed. They were back at Marissa's house after the Christmas Tree Festival. The moment he'd walked in the door, he'd headed for the shower, and now he was dressed in sweatpants and a T-shirt. The only reason he'd come back out into the living room was because Marissa had offered to make them a mug of hot chocolate.

"Cool." She gave him a shy smile as she placed the mugs on the coffee table. "You pick something. I'm going to get the fire started."

Danny watched Marissa fiddle with the fireplace, wondering if he'd manifested this moment. Hadn't he just been thinking about watching Christmas movies before he'd gone to the festival? He picked up the remote and flipped the station to one that he knew was playing Christmas movies 24/7 through the new year.

Marissa glanced up at the screen and then turned and raised her eyebrows at him. "Did you really just pick something called *Small Town Christmas?*"

He chuckled softly as he took a seat on the couch. "It seemed appropriate."

Her eyes twinkled as she smiled softly at him. "You're right, it does. What else would Mr. Garland watch after becoming the town hero at the local Christmas festival?"

"Stop." He rolled his eyes, but there was no denying he was loving their interaction.

Pumpkin came running in from the kitchen and bounded up onto the couch next to him. She snuggled in close, putting her head underneath his hand, begging to have her ears scratched. He gave in, giving her what she wanted as she melted as if she were boneless.

"My dog is going to switch loyalties if you keep that up," she said, smiling down at them.

"The way my cat is now convinced she's supposed to sleep in your room?" he asked. For the past few nights, Bells had come into his room, gotten the pets she'd demanded and then left for the night. Danny had thought maybe she just liked sleeping on the couch or curled up in the chair, but that morning, he'd caught her stretching as she strolled out of Marissa's room looking as if she'd just had the best catnap of her life.

"She likes the fuzzy blanket I have at the end of the bed." Marissa covered her mouth, trying to hide a giggle.

"So that's the secret? I just need to up my blanket game?" he asked.

"Looks like it."

He wanted to say it would be easier to just climb into her bed, since his cat had already staked out territory there, but he kept that thought to himself. He didn't want to ruin whatever this was between them before they even got started.

Once the fire was roaring, Marissa stood, looked at the chair she usually sat in and then eyed Danny and Pumpkin. "I guess turnabout is fair play, huh? Your cat likes to sleep with me, and my dog is an attention whore with you."

He let out a bark of laughter. "It appears we've both been thrown over for the other. Tell you what, why don't you sit with us, and that way Pumpkin gets the attention she deserves."

"Sit with you for Pumpkin's sake, huh?" She raised one eyebrow. "That's seems convenient."

"It does, doesn't it?" He winked at her as he patted the couch cushion beside him and the pup.

Wearing an amused smile, she grabbed her hot chocolate and then curled up beside them.

Danny continued to pet Pumpkin, and when Marissa placed her hand on the pup, their fingers brushed, sending an electric shock up his arm. Neither of them moved their hands away as their eyes met.

Finally Marissa glanced away and focused on the

television. Without looking at him, she said, "It's almost like old times."

"Is it?" He wasn't so sure. "The last time we watched a movie together, I seem to recall you wanted to watch an ice skating movie and I wanted to watch the latest Batman flick. Neither of us were happy when we settled on some foreign film that didn't interest either one of us."

"You remember that?" Marissa asked, looking a little shocked. "I thought for sure you'd blocked that out. Those dubbed titles were horrible!"

"They were. And we were both so stubborn, each trying to get our way." He snorted out a laugh. "Imagine spending our one night off together arguing about what type of movie to watch."

"Is that why you just put this on?" Marissa waved a hand at the television. "You just decided to give in before the argument happened?"

"No, not at all." Danny reached over and brushed a lock of hair out of her eyes. "Believe it or not, I actually enjoy these feel-good movies these days. Do I still like action films? Of course, but after spending time in Christmas Grove, I've learned to enjoy the magic that comes from the quiet moments." He stared into her quizzical eyes. "I'm not sure one can live in Christmas Grove and remain cynical."

It was her turn to laugh. "Oh, I think it's possible. It's just harder when there are dancing snowmen and sugar plum fairies roaming about."

"I am really enjoying my time here, staying with you," Danny said, deciding it was best to just let it all out. "I wish our schedules were a little more aligned, but I like making you coffee in the morning and coming home to whatever you've made for dinner that day." He glanced down at the fluffy dog cuddling between them. "And I especially enjoy this sweet little monster."

"Pumpkin is the best part of my day," she said, gazing lovingly at her pooch.

"And here I thought I might be the best part of your day." Danny clutched at his heart dramatically. "I'm wounded."

Marissa rolled her eyes. But then she sobered. "I used to think that, you know. Back when we were married. I used to tell my friends that you were the best thing that ever happened to me."

"You used to think that?" He raised his eyebrows in question. "You mean I wasn't?"

Marissa moved away, causing him to drop his hand that had been caressing her cheek. "No, you were. But..." She blew out a breath. "Don't take this the wrong way, but after you left, I realized that we'd been doing a lot of fighting."

"It was hard because we didn't have a lot of time to spend together," he said, feeling a little defensive. He'd tried his best. He'd left because he loved her so much.

"I know." Marissa met and held his gaze. "But we were so young and had no idea who we were without each other. Or who we were as a couple. Did we do anything together? Did we take care of each other like we are now?"

"That's just because we didn't know how to do that yet," he said.

"That's not true. You knew how to take care of me when it mattered. You did leave to keep me safe." She gave him a pained smile. "But were we making coffee for each other or thinking to leave meals when the other was working or at school? You weren't putting on movies you thought I'd like, and I certainly wasn't interested in the movies you watched. We were just on two totally different pages."

"Are you saying our marriage was a mistake?" he asked, feeling as if his heart was about to crack. Was this where she told him that despite everything, she was happy with the way things turned out?

"No." She shook her head, looking pained. "Not at all. I'm saying that we didn't have a chance in hell back then. And that all this time I've been blaming you for what happened, when maybe that's not completely fair. I wasn't taking care of you at all, was I?"

"You were busy with school and work," he offered, but he knew what she was talking about. He'd always been looking out for her safety. The visions had been intense, and it was all he could do to warn her, to make sure she didn't get hurt. But everything else? It was a struggle. Who was going to cook? Who was going to clean up? Pay the bills? Do the shopping? Plan their date night? Everything was a struggle, and gone were the days when they'd just hung out on the back porch, enjoying talking about anything and everything when they'd just been kids. Once they'd gotten married and took on the burden of being a couple, they'd lost a lot of who they were.

"We were nineteen, Danny," she said gently. "Didn't

Sophie say the way to break the curse was to learn to trust each other?"

"Yes."

"This is how we learn to trust each other. By being honest about what happened. The curse was the catalyst that led to you leaving, but I honestly don't know what would have happened if we'd never been cursed. Would we have made it?"

He reached over and threaded his fingers between hers, holding her one hand with both of his. "I honestly hope we would have."

"So do I," she said, tears standing in her eyes. "I like to think that we were so close that we'd have eventually figured it out. But when I see how effortlessly we've fallen into a life together here at my house, I can't help but wonder what would have become of us."

"We were just kids," he said. "It's no wonder we were still trying to figure out who we were as individuals. I think we'd have eventually gotten there."

"Maybe. I guess it's just stark because I see everything you do for me, and it makes me feel terrible that I wasn't doing things to make your day easier back then. I hope I am now."

"You are." He smiled at her. "Dinner every night? You're a goddess for that."

"You make me coffee every morning. And you do dishes and unload the dishwasher before I get home every day."

"You change Bells's water bowl and clean her litter box while I'm at work," he said.

"I just scoop it out for her. She likes a fresh box," Marissa said with a shrug.

He laughed. "Yes, she does. Thank you."

"Thank you for keeping me safe." Her expression was serious and full of emotion. "You're the best man I know, Danny Frost. I think it's important that you know that."

"And you, Marissa Cane, are the most loyal, determined, loving person I've ever known. And I'd be lying if I said I didn't miss you."

Marissa blinked back the tears that were standing in her eyes and then she leaned in and pressed her palm against his cheek. In barely a whisper, she said, "Kiss me, Danny."

CHAPTER 17

*W*hat are you doing? What are you doing? What are you doing? The words just kept repeating in Marissa's head as she pressed her lips to Danny's and felt a rush of familiarity, but also something completely new. Danny had an air of confidence that she didn't remember. His hands were cupping her face as his mouth claimed hers, kissing her as if he'd been dying to taste her for months.

Months? She almost laughed. More like years.

How many times had she dreamed of this happening? Of Danny coming back into her life and the two of them picking up as if nothing had ever happened. She'd always imagined him sweeping her off her feet and taking her to her bedroom to show her just how sorry he was for ever even considering leaving her.

But in her dreams, she hadn't realized just how much she'd wanted him. How scared she was to give herself over to this man who'd hurt her deeply. Or that no matter how many times she told herself to take it slow, she just couldn't pull away from him.

There was a desperation in his touch. The same desperation that radiated from her very core. This man was hers. He always had been. And she was certain that no matter how long she lived, he'd always be the one for her.

Marissa didn't know how long they sat on her couch kissing. All she knew was that she wanted more. Wanted him. Finally, when they were both breathing heavily, she stood and held her hand out to him.

Danny looked up at her, all the questions in his eyes. "Are you sure?"

"I'm sure," she said and then led him to her bedroom.

And when he laid her down in her bed and crawled over her, she felt it in her bones that her Danny was finally home.

MARISSA WOKE to the scent of coffee and a hint of cinnamon. She pried her eyelids apart and blinked away the sleep in her eyes. When she saw Danny smiling down at her, she couldn't help reaching for him. "Why are you up?"

He chuckled. "That pesky thing called work. I have orders to fill and a private lesson later this afternoon."

"Nooooo. You should be right here next to me. Preferably naked." She pumped her eyebrows, knowing there was zero hope of getting him back into her bed before he left for work. But it was fun to watch his face flush as she flirted with him.

"You know I can't. But I brought you coffee and a freshly baked cinnamon roll."

"You *baked*?" she asked, pushing herself up into a sitting position.

He laughed. "Why do you say that like it's impossible?"

"It's not. I mean, I don't think that at all. It's just so early. What time did you get up to make these? And why… when you could have woken me up and we could've spent some more time getting reacquainted?"

"Do you really think I got up one minute earlier than I had to this morning? Especially when I had all of that in my arms?" He let his gaze roam over her torso, not bothering to hide his appreciation.

"So where did the cinnamon rolls come from?" she asked.

"Would you believe that Felicity dropped them off?"

"No. Absolutely not." Marissa shook her head. "Felicity never bakes at home. It's because she spends so much time around all the apple pies and turnovers at work."

"I hate to break it to you, but it was indeed your friend Felicity. She also told me to tell you that she expects a full review before you go into work tonight." He paused and then added, "Considering the way she was looking at me, I'm guessing she's not talking about a review of the cinnamon rolls, is she?"

Marissa laughed, just imagining the look on Felicity's face. "I'd guess not, but what did you do, answer the door naked?"

He sputtered. "Of course not. I was wearing sweatpants. But I think this may have given it away." He pulled his shirt down just enough to show her a small red mark on his collarbone.

"Oh, oops." She giggled and knew her friends were going to embarrass her something terrible when they came into the pub later that day. But she knew their teasing would be all in good fun and that they'd be happy for her. "I think perhaps I got a little carried away. Sorry about that."

"Don't you dare apologize," he ordered and then went in for a kiss.

When they finally came up for air, he stood and backed away. "I have to go or else I'm never gonna leave."

"That wouldn't bother me one bit." She picked up the coffee and took a long sip. "No one is waiting for you at the shop, right?"

"Oh no, evil witch. If I climb into that bed, neither of us will be going anywhere for hours." He backed up further. "I'll come by the pub after work. How about that?"

"It's not the same," she said with a fake pout. "But I'll be looking forward to it anyway."

She watched him hesitate in the doorway, and then as if he'd been having an argument with himself, he finally let out a breath, strode over to her, gave her one last kiss, and then disappeared.

Pumpkin darted after him, barking her displeasure when the front door slammed and the roar of the truck filled the silence. A few moments later, Pumpkin trotted back into the room and jumped up on the bed. She curled up next to Bells, looking forlorn as she stared at the door where he'd been only moments before.

"You and me both, sister," Marissa said as she leaned back to enjoy her coffee and pastry in bed. Smiling to herself, she decided that waking up to a hot man, hot coffee, and a warm pastry might be the perfect way to start her day.

Just as she finished the last bite of the cinnamon roll, there was loud knocking on the door, followed by her phone buzzing with a text.

Felicity: *We saw him leave. Get your butt out of bed. We have questions.*

Marissa groaned and wondered who thought it was a good idea to live next door to the nosy sisters. She looked at Pumpkin and Bells and said, "You two have now been promoted to favorite status."

Pumpkin just looked at her with a bored expression.

"Yeah, okay, you were already at favorite status, but it's even more so now. Come on. Your aunties aren't gonna go away until they get the deets."

Marissa pulled on her pajamas and wrapped herself in a robe before she and Pumpkin went to answer the door. She glanced back at Bells, who had curled up and gone back to sleep, and wondered if it was wrong to be jealous of a cat.

With a huff, she pulled the door open and was almost knocked over by her friends barging right into her house.

"Come on in, why don't you," she said dryly before closing the door and making a beeline for the kitchen. This was going to require a lot more coffee.

"How was he?" Felicity asked without any preamble.

"Felicity!" Clara admonished. "That was crass. You're supposed to ask how her evening was. And it if extended into this morning."

Marissa shook her head at her friends. "You two are up entirely too early."

"It's eight," Clara said, sounding as if interrogating your friend about her love life first thing in the morning was perfectly reasonable. "So you did it?"

Felicity rolled her eyes. "Of course they did it. Look at her." The tall blonde let out an envious sigh. "She looks like she's been ravished. You know, Danny is hot, but I kinda thought he was too sweet for all of this." She waved a hand up and down at Marissa. "But judging by the look on your face, I'd say sweet wasn't exactly on the agenda last night."

"It was sweet when we were watching *Small Town Christmas*," Marissa offered.

"Don't tell me you put that on and made that man watch it." Felicity looked like someone had just suggested that she eat week-old sushi.

"He watched *Small Town Christmas* with you?" Clara asked, placing her hand over her heart. "That is really romantic."

"It's not exactly how I'd entice someone into my bed, but it looks like maybe he was desperate enough that he was willing to put up with that BS just to get you under the sheets." Felicity wrinkled her nose. "He's a better man than me, because if any guy put that on, I'd show him the door."

"You would not," Marissa said, knowing her friend secretly loved Christmas movies. "I've caught you watching *Her Christmas Prince* more than once."

"Not while on a date!" Felicity threw her hands up. "Have I taught you nothing?"

"It's a good thing it wasn't a date then, isn't it?" Marissa said. "And he was the one who put the movie on. Not me. One thing led to another and... Well, here we are." She gave her friends what she knew must've been a sappy grin.

"That's just..." Clara blinked back happy tears. "I love a second-chance romance."

Felicity sat back, looking stunned, and then threw her head back and laughed. "Okay. Props to Danny. That man has moves."

"I don't think it was moves. I mean, I don't think any of it was premeditated. We just... I don't know. I think we were just finally honest with one another and now we're... whatever this is."

"He's your lobster," Clara said, her eyes gleaming as she referenced her favorite *Friends* episode.

"Not this again." Felicity rolled her eyes. "He's just a man who wanted to get laid. We'll know more once we see what he does next."

Marissa just listened to her friends try to analyze her relationship with Danny. She knew in her heart that he loved her, and while she didn't want to jinx it, she figured Clara was right. Danny *was* her lobster, and she was ready to do whatever it took to keep him in her life.

CHAPTER 18

*D*anny was smiling to himself as he walked into Sleighed that evening. In fact, he'd been smiling all day. When he'd gotten up the day before, he hadn't had an inkling that there'd be such a major turn of events in his life. He'd regretted how he'd handled things with Marissa, had dreamed about once again being with her for years, and now just like that, she was his again. He'd be damned if he messed it up this time.

A small cheer went up from the end of the bar, where he spotted Clara and Felicity nursing a couple of beers.

"Stop it," Marissa said to her friends as she slipped out from behind the bar and came to wrap her arms around him.

He smiled down at her. "It's like this now? You're ready for the entire town to know that we're together?"

She nodded and pressed up on her tiptoes to give him a kiss.

He claimed her lips and made a show of dipping her backward, playing up the interaction so that there was no confusion. Marissa Cane was his, and he wanted everyone to know it.

When the applause started, he put her back on her feet and they grinned at each other.

"How was your day?" Marissa asked him as she led him to the bar.

"Good. Though I need to go back and spend some time on the wheel before I go home for the night. Most of the day was spent in the gallery. I think half the town showed up today."

"Everyone wants a piece of Mr. Garland," she teased.

"Too bad all my pieces are reserved for you and only you," he said.

"Awww," Clara said.

"Gross," Felicity added.

Everyone laughed, including Marissa and Danny.

Marissa retreated back behind the bar and leaned over to ask him, "Are you hungry?"

He let his gaze roam over her, making it clear he was hungry for something other than food.

"Get a room!" Felicity called out.

"Gladly," Danny whispered to Marissa. "When can you ditch this joint?"

"Not until closing time, unfortunately. But at least it's a weekday. I should be able to get out of here by ten thirty or eleven."

He groaned. That was later than he hoped, but at least he'd be able to get some work done in the studio. "Okay, food it is then." He placed an order for a burger and fries and sat back to enjoy his beer while he watched Marissa interact with her customers.

Sleighed was both a local favorite and a place where transients came for the evening to enjoy a bit of the local flavor. It was nice to see the locals embracing them, giving suggestions on what to do in Christmas Grove over the holidays and generally making them feel welcome. It was all part of the magical fabric of the town, and one of the reasons he'd decided to move to Christmas Grove.

He couldn't remember when he'd ever been as content as he was in that very moment.

"It looks like things are going well," a familiar voice said from beside him.

He startled as he glanced at the ethereal sugar plum fairy that was sitting next to him. Had she just popped in out of nowhere? Danny wasn't sure, but he wasn't ruling it out. Today she was wearing a shimmering cream dress with elaborate lace-up, knee-high boots.

Danny took a sip of his beer. "Things are going well. And the incidents seem to have calmed down significantly since I've moved in with Marissa."

"Excellent." She snapped her fingers, making her own beer appear in front of her. She picked it up and clinked her glass to his. "Hopefully this means I'll have my wings by Christmas."

He eyed the woman. "I just have to ask, what more do we need to do to make sure this curse is broken for good?"

"Once you trust one another again, the curse will be broken," she said.

"Yeah, I heard you the first time you said that. When will we know we're there?"

"You'll know." She gave him a wan smile and downed her beer. Then she glanced around the bar, spotted a couple at a table, and said, "Excuse me. I see a young couple who needs a little help." As she slid off her stool, she patted him on the arm and added, "Good work, Danny. If you keep it up, she'll let go of her resentment in no time."

Her resentment? Did Marissa resent him? Was she still upset about him leaving? He knew he couldn't expect her to forgive and forget overnight, but she certainly seemed to be moving past it all.

She glanced up from where she was mixing a drink and flashed that radiant smile at him.

His insides lit with warmth every time she looked at him like that. He saw both the young woman he'd fallen in love with all those years ago as well as the confident force of nature he was still getting to know. He knew deep down that he loved everything about her, and if she let him, he'd love her for the rest of their days. He wouldn't be scared away this time. This time he'd fight, no matter what came their way.

"Hey, man," Jackson said as he placed the burger and fries in front of Danny. "I hear congratulations are in order." He glanced at Marissa and then back at Danny. "The boss lady certainly seems happy about this new development."

"She's not the only one," Danny said.

"Glad to hear it." Jackson patted him on the shoulder

and then headed back to the kitchen, but he paused at the other end of the bar as he leaned in to say something to Felicity.

She gave him a flirty smile before grabbing him by his chef's whites and pulling him in closer so she could whisper in his ear.

Marissa appeared in front of him. "Something wrong with the burger?"

He glanced at his untouched plate and chuckled. "No idea. I haven't even tasted it yet. Is there something going on with Felicity and Jackson?"

She followed his gaze to the end of the bar before shaking her head. "Nah. Felicity just likes to flirt with him. She always has ever since he started working here. I guess she's wearing him down because he used to just be polite, but now he's leaning into it. Can't blame him, really. Felicity is a lot of fun to be around."

Danny nodded. Though he wasn't quite as convinced as Marissa that the two didn't have a thing for each other. He could see Jackson with someone like Felicity. Even though he was a stoic friend, he was also a thrill seeker. Felicity was the perfect woman to keep someone on their toes. "I think they'd be good together."

"You think so?" Marissa frowned at them. "But Jackson is just so... steady. And Felicity, she's kind of like a bull in a China shop some days with those opinions of hers. I love her to death, but easygoing isn't in her vocabulary."

He chuckled. "You're right. Jackson is steady. He's also got a strong center. It kind of sounds like they might be the perfect match."

Marissa paused to think about that for a moment. Then she nodded and said, "You know what? I think you might be right about that. The only problem is that I don't think Felicity has ever been interested in a long-term relationship, and I'd hate to have drama between them. Hopefully they just stick to flirting."

As Danny watched the pair in question, their heads tilted together as they talked, he thought, *yeah, good luck with that one.*

By the time Danny was done eating, the bar was hopping and it was time for him to get back to work. He left money with a generous tip on the bar and stood to leave, but just as he got to his feet, his world shifted and he had a vision of a person driving while talking on their phone, then they lost control of their car and ran right into the front of Sleighed.

The vision cleared just as quickly as it appeared, and when he was oriented again, he ran outside of the bar, his hands high in the air as he waved at the car that was still a few blocks down the street.

"Stop!" he shouted, knowing they couldn't hear him. He ran to his 4Runner that was parked a few doors down and laid on the horn. Then he started the vehicle and slammed it into Reverse. As quickly as he could, he turned the car so that the headlights were aimed right at the offending car.

The SUV swerved, just like Danny had hoped, and instead of hitting the bar and hurting all the people he cared about inside, the SUV slammed into the right side of his 4Runner, spinning his truck around until he crashed right into a utility pole.

Danny's head swam as a woman appeared. One he hadn't seen in sixteen years.

Patience peered at him from the passenger's seat. Her dark hair was pulled into a severe bun, and her bright red lips were pursed in a pucker as she looked him over.

"What are you doing here?" he asked, breathing through the pain that was radiating up from his left ankle.

"I told you once before that if you didn't stay away from Marissa you were going to end up hurting her. This is your warning. Leave Christmas Grove now, or next time, this will be her."

As the sound of sirens filled the air, the woman vanished and coldness set in.

CHAPTER 19

*M*arissa's heart was pounding as she ran out of Sleighed just in time to see the dark SUV slam into Danny's 4Runner. Everything seemed to slow down, and she felt like she was watching in slow motion as the truck spun around and then crashed into the light pole. She was frozen, in complete shock as she watched the dark SUV back up and then slam on the gas as they tried to hightail it away from the accident.

Immediately, she pulled out her phone and started taking pictures, praying that somewhere in there, they'd be able to make out the license plate. Once the SUV was gone, she turned and ran to Danny's 4Runner while sirens blared from a few streets over. Good. Someone had called 911.

When the driver's side door wouldn't budge, she hurried to the passenger side and climbed in. "Danny?"

He blinked and then looked at her. "Marissa?"

"Oh gods. You're hurt. Your head is bleeding." She reached out to touch his forehead, to try to inspect his wound, but thought better of it and pulled her hand back. She didn't want to make anything worse.

"Where is she?" he asked. "Is she still here? Stay away from her. She's dangerous."

"She? Who's she? Who's dangerous?" Marissa scanned the area. When she didn't see anyone, she assumed he was talking about the driver of the other car. "No one is here, Danny. It's just me. Marissa."

He placed a hand on her cheek and looked right at her as he said," I won't leave."

"I won't either, babe. I'm here."

Her door swung open and one of the paramedics poked his head in. "Marissa? What happened? Are you hurt?"

Marissa shook her head and peered through the darkness at Jake Jamison, one of her regulars. "I'm fine. I wasn't in the truck when the accident happened. I just came to check on Danny. He has a cut on his forehead and seems to be a little confused, but otherwise, he was talking just a minute ago. I'm not sure what else might be hurt."

"Okay. We'll take it from here. Do you want to ride to the hospital with us?" Jake asked.

"I'll drive. I'll want my car later," she said, slipping out of the 4Runner and feeling completely helpless while they pried the driver's side door open.

"Mar?" Clara said, coming up behind her and placing her jacket over her shoulders. "I'm going to close up the bar, okay?"

She nodded, still staring at the truck, waiting for them to get Danny free.

"I'm going to grab your keys from your purse. Is that all right?" Clara asked.

"Of course." She looked at her friend, saw the concern there, and quickly glanced away. "He's fine. He'll be fine."

"Of course he will," she said. "Wait for us. We'll drive you to the hospital."

"But my car—"

"One of us will drive it there so you'll have it," she said. "Just promise you won't leave without one of us taking you. Okay?"

Marissa nodded and let out a tiny gasp when they finally got the driver's side door open and started to tug Danny out of the truck. His eyes were closed, and he looked unconscious.

"They'll take good care of him," Clara said as she squeezed Marissa's hand.

The moment Clara went back inside, Felicity appeared. She didn't say anything; she just held Marissa's hand while they waited for Danny to get loaded into the ambulance. Once they shut the door and took off down the street, Felicity tugged on Marissa's hand. "Let's go. I'll drive."

Marissa didn't argue. She just got into Felicity's Jeep and stared straight ahead as a light snow began to fall. It was almost like a cleansing as the white snow blanketed the town. But she knew it was just a mask, as Danny was still hurt, and until she was certain he was going to be all right, there would be no cleansing of anything.

～

THE HARSH LIGHTS of the emergency waiting room grated on Marissa's nerves. She, Felicity, and Clara had been waiting in the hard plastic chairs for over two hours. Zach had arrived about an hour earlier and was in talking to the doctor, finally. But Atlas was out of town, doing a Christmas special. Zach told him he'd call when he had news.

"I'm sure he's going to be fine," Clara said for about the tenth time.

Marissa just nodded. She'd been praying to the goddesses since they'd gotten there. Surely one of them was listening.

The door swung open, and Zach appeared, heading straight for Marissa. "He's asking for you."

She stood and clutched at his arm. "How is he?"

"A little banged up, but the doctor says he should be fine. They are watching him for signs of a concussion, and he'll be in a walking cast for a while. It appears he has a fracture in his left ankle."

"And the cut on his head? Did he need stitches?" she asked.

"No. They put some of that skin glue on that wound and said it should heal within a few days."

She let out a long breath. "That's all good news, right?"

"All good news." Zach walked her to the door of Danny's room and said, "Maybe this isn't the right time to ask, but since you're here and Danny's asking for you, does that mean you two are trying to put your relationship back together?"

She nodded. "Yes. We're..." She shrugged. "He's been staying at my house." It wasn't an explanation, but it was enough to get the point across. "When he leaves, he'll come home with me."

"I see," he said with a nod. "That's good. Very good actually."

"Thank you, Zach," she said, hugging him. "I've been worried sick."

"I can see that." He smiled gently at her. "He's just as worried about you."

"Me? Why me?" She stared at him, her eyes wide. "I'm not the one who was spun around like an amusement park ride in my car."

"I'm not sure. He kept asking if you're okay. Maybe he thought you were with him in his vehicle."

If that was true, Marissa wasn't reassured about his condition. If he couldn't even remember that he was by himself, then he definitely wasn't okay.

"I'm going to head to the lobby and call Atlas to give him an update. Let Danny know I'm still here if he needs anything." Zach squeezed her hand and then strode down the hall.

Marissa sucked in a deep breath and walked into the room.

Danny's eyes lit up when he saw her. "There you are. Zach said you were here, but since I hadn't seen you, I wondered if you'd already left."

She moved to sit on the side of his bed, taking his hand

in hers. "You think I would've left without making sure you're okay with my own two eyes?"

"No. Not really." He lifted her hand and kissed her knuckles. "I have a broken ankle."

"I heard. That's one way of getting out of doing the dishes for the next month," she teased.

He smiled at her. "Just get me a stool. I'll still load the dishwasher."

"How are you feeling? Do you have much pain? A headache?"

"Not really. The ankle hurts when I move it. My head, there's a dull ache where the cut is, but other than just feeling overall a little beat up, I think I'm okay. What about you?"

She frowned at him. "I'm fine. Why wouldn't I be?"

His expression turned dark before he blinked and grimaced slightly. "I went out there because I had a vision of that SUV hitting Sleighed. I didn't intend to become the target instead, but it appears that was the outcome. I just wanted to make sure no one else got hurt." He caressed her fingers. "Especially you."

"At least that explains what you were doing out there when I thought you were going back to the studio," she said. Then very gently, she added, "Thank you for trying to stop that tragedy, but I'd appreciate it if you kept yourself safe next time."

He let out a small snort of humorless laughter. "Believe me, I plan to do just that. How's my 4Runner? Totaled, or does it look like it can be fixed?"

"I'm no expert in body shop work, but if I had to guess, I'd bet you're going car shopping for the new year."

He groaned. "Maybe there will be good deals as the dealers try to move inventory."

She nodded, unable to shake the feeling that something was very off. It wasn't that Danny was hurt and in the hospital, though that certainly was quite troubling. It was something else. Something she couldn't quite put her finger on. "I'm sure something will pop up. Until then, we can share my car."

"That's very kind of you," he said, closing his eyes.

She chuckled softly. "I plan to continue sharing my house and bed with you. The car is nothing."

His lips twitched with amusement, though he didn't open his eyes. "This isn't exactly how I planned my evening. Do you think they'll let me out of here anytime soon?"

That was a good question. "If you have a concussion, probably not. But let me go find out. I'll be right back."

"I'll be counting on it."

Marissa gave him a light kiss on the cheek and then went out to find one of the doctors. The hallway was eerily quiet, without a soul to be found. It was late, but it was also the emergency room. Didn't that mean the place was usually pretty hectic?

When she found the nurses desk, no one was there. She glanced around, looking for someone, anyone, when she felt someone brush up against her arm. Marissa spun and then jumped back a step when she found a woman standing right next to her. She had dark hair that was pulled back into a severe bun and was wearing bright red lipstick. Her black lace dress and black leather boots made her stick out like a sore thumb. Clearly, she wasn't one of the doctors or nurses.

"Have you seen the doctor?" Marissa asked her.

"Sure. He's busy taking care of some woman who is short of breath." The woman was staring intently at Marissa as if sizing her up. But for what? Marissa had no idea.

"Okay. Thanks. I'm going to go see if I can find the nurse."

As she started to walk away, the woman's cold hand wrapped around Marissa's wrist, stopping her. "You're not going to find the nurse either. Not until I say so, anyway."

Marissa looked down at the woman's blood-red nails that were pinching her skin and yanked her arm away from her. "Who are you?"

The woman gave Marissa a thin smile that looked more like it belonged on a deranged cat. "Patience. I'd say it's nice to finally meet you, Marissa, but this day was never supposed to come. If Danny had stuck with the plan, none of this would have ever happened." She waved toward Danny's room. "See what happens when someone disobeys?"

"*Patience?*" Marissa spat out. "Sophie's sister? The one who cursed Danny!"

The woman smirked. "You can yell and carry on all you like. No one will hear you. At least not while I'm here. But yes, that's me. Patience, the fallen sugar plum fairy."

"What do you want with us? Sophie said you were in

love with Danny, but he hasn't seen or spoken to you in sixteen years. Why are you so invested in torturing us? Is this *fun* for you?"

"Well, yes, it does make the days more interesting. But that's not the real reason. You see, Sophie forgot to tell you the most important part of the equation. Fallen sugar plum fairies get their power from broken men. We feed on it. So the unhappier they are, the better off we are. Get it now? Sophie's solution is so naive. 'Just learn to love and trust each other and the spell will be broken.' Hardly!" She threw her head back and laughed. "The more you try to stay together, the worse the curse will get until one or both of you ends up right back here. My warning to you is to stay away from Danny Frost, or your worst nightmare might just come true."

Marissa wanted to strangle the fallen fairy right there at the nurse's desk. "You're the reason his visions are coming on stronger and stronger. Are you setting these awful accidents in motion, too?"

Patience shrugged.

"Do you really think you can keep me and Danny apart? It's not going to work. Not this time. We're not going to let you take anything else from us, do you understand? You're a sad and pathetic being that has nothing good to live for." Everything inside of Marissa screamed for her to spit on the evil being, but she kept herself in check. Having a cat fight in the hospital wouldn't solve anything. "I actually pity you."

"Pity me all you want. It won't change anything. Stay away from Danny or suffer the consequences."

The lights flickered, and suddenly the hallway was full of activity again. The nurses were bustling about, and the doctor was headed straight for Marissa.

Patience turned and walked down the hall, but not before Marissa noticed a small but distinct limp. Marissa wanted to run after the rancid fairy and sweep her leg out from beneath her, stomp on her leg, and leave a mark the way Patience had when she'd caused Danny's accident.

But Marissa was pulled from her dark fantasy when the doctor said, "We've cleared Danny to go home as long as he has someone to keep an eye out for a possible concussion."

"I can do that," she said and decided she could deal with Patience later.

Once the paperwork was done, Marissa went back into Danny's room. His eyes were closed, and he appeared to be sleeping peacefully. She wanted to curl up next to him. Promise him that none of this would happen again. That he wouldn't be stuck for the rest of his life trying to save her from some curse. That they'd be a normal couple, just like everyone else.

But she couldn't because she had no idea if that was true. Sophie had told them that if they spent time together and learned to trust each other again, then the curse would be broken. They'd done that, hadn't they? She'd given herself to him the night before. And he'd given himself to her. There was no question about that.

And the fact was, that in order for Marissa to share her bed with Danny, she had to trust him. When it came to him, her heart was too fragile to go there unless she was sure he wouldn't hurt her again.

So why was the curse still hanging over them? Why had Patience come to warn her that this would only get worse if they didn't separate? Who was right? And who exactly could she ask? Sugar plum fairies weren't exactly an everyday occurrence. She doubted that anyone in town had ever dealt with one.

She walked over to the bed and sat next to Danny. Could she keep doing this? Keep letting him save her and risk himself due to all these so-called accidents? For the first time since he'd left her all those years ago, Marissa was starting to understand why he'd left. And more importantly, why he'd left without explaining.

Her heart ached for the boy who'd made that decision. It ached for the girl who'd been so hurt and lost for so many years afterward. And it ached for them both and the choice they'd undoubtedly have to make, probably sooner rather than later.

"Hey. How long have you been here?" he asked, blinking up at her.

"Just a minute. The doctor says you're free to go." She entwined her fingers with his. "You just have to agree to let me check on you every few hours to make sure that head of yours is doing okay."

"I'm more than happy to do that." He tugged on her hand. "Come down here a minute."

She did as he asked and then grinned as he kissed her. "I guess you are feeling better."

"Definitely."

CHAPTER 20

"*I* can do it," Danny said as he hobbled around the kitchen on his crutches, determined to make his own coffee even if it was one-handed.

"I know you can," Marissa said, shaking her head at him. "But why should you have to when you have your beck-and-call girl here?"

"You're hovering again," he said, raising his eyebrow at her. He'd been back at her house for days now. And while he appreciated all of her help, he was ready to get on with a life where he wasn't just lying in bed being waited on hand and foot.

Marissa held her hands up and took a step back. "Sorry. Didn't mean to smother."

"I meant to tell you that Zach found a golf cart today for us to use," Danny said, turning around and leaning against the counter, his mug in hand.

Her eyes lit up, making her look happier than she had

in days. Ever since the accident, Marissa had been subdued. Not quite herself. At first, he'd chalked it up to her being worried about him, but now he wasn't so sure. Was she having second thoughts? Was she regretting letting him stay with her? He'd definitely been a burden to her. Not only had she been cooking and cleaning up after him, but she'd also insisted on going into work with him to help in the gallery while he finished his custom orders that he had to get done in time for Christmas.

It was no wonder she was tired of him.

He knew it was a lot to deal with when they were just getting to know each other again. He just hoped that he hadn't scared her off. Because now that he had her back in his life, he wasn't sure he could handle letting her go.

"Your cousin is amazing. Remind me to tell him the next time he comes into Sleighed that the drinks are on me." She glanced down at Pumpkin. "Did you hear that, girl? Looks like Danny is going to be able to accompany us to the Paw-mas parade after all."

Pumpkin let out a bark of approval and then ran around in a circle, demonstrating her pleasure.

Danny laughed at her. "Do you want to be a reindeer or an elf this year, Pumpkin?"

The dog looked up at him with a quizzical expression, making him laugh harder. "Reindeer it is." He held the dog outfit up and said, "You're going to be the best dressed with that scarf your mommy made for you."

Marissa was looking at him with amusement in her eyes. "I can't believe you're so into this. Clara and Felicity told me I'm on my own with this one."

"Who doesn't want to participate in a Christmas dog parade? What is wrong with your friends?"

"Oh, they want to participate, only they want to do it from the bar as they watch the puppies go by. They don't want to walk in it. Of course, they turned me down before they knew we'd have a golf cart, so that's their loss."

"Do either of them have a dog?" Danny asked.

"No, but we have Pumpkin." Marissa reached down and picked up her pup. "She'd be more than happy to have more than just us as handlers. Wouldn't you, girl?"

Pumpkin gave her a big kiss, licking half her face.

Danny laughed. "That right there might explain a few things. Not everyone wants to bathe in dog kisses."

"What?" she cried in mock surprise and then laughed as she put Pumpkin down. "You might be onto something. Anyway, let me get Pumpkin dressed and then we'll be ready to go. Do you need anything first?"

"Nope. Not a thing. I have my crutches and one good leg. I'll manage."

Her lips curved down into the tiniest frown as she narrowed her eyes slightly, and he couldn't help but wonder once again what was bothering her.

"I'm fine. Really," he said again.

She nodded once. "I know. I do." Then she forced a smile before she headed for the hallway, calling for Pumpkin to join her.

～

"OH. EM. GEE!" Marissa exclaimed. "Just look at how cute everyone is."

Danny glanced at her and didn't miss the heart eyes she had for all the puppies that were lined up along Main Street just waiting for the Paw-mas parade to start. Not only did the parade include dogs, along with their humans, dressed up as everything Christmas, but the people who came to watch also brought their dogs and dressed them up, putting in as much, if not more, care for their costumes as the parade walkers did.

"This is fantastic," Danny said, steering the cart his cousin had secured for them into the line behind the other parade participants that had chosen eclectic vehicles. The line was broken up into walkers and riders, and then the coordinators would indicate which would go at which time so that the parade itself was intermixed with both on a regular basis. "I can't believe I never knew about this."

"It's mostly a locals thing," Marissa said. "Some tourists show up for it each year, but one has to be a resident of Christmas Grove to be a part of the parade. That's what keeps it from becoming commercialized. Otherwise, can't you just imagine this parade being broadcast every year right after the annual dog show?

"Doesn't that happen on Thanksgiving?" he asked.

"Yeah. And they'd make us move this just so they could air it to that captive audience."

"Okay," he said, chuckling. That sounded a little dramatic, but it wouldn't be the first time some producer had decided it was time to capitalize on the wonders of Christmas Grove.

"Look," Marissa said, pointing to the golf cart in front of them. "That Lab is dressed up like a Christmas tree." Her voice went very high pitched as she added, "Look at the red balls hanging off his tail."

"He's lucky that's the only place they're hanging from," Zach said as he strode up to them. "Mia, my daughter, tried to tied them to his ears, too." He snapped his fingers and the dog in question hopped off the cart and came running. He sat obediently at Zach's feet, his tongue lolling out. "Danny, meet Spruce. The best dog in the world, who should earn a medal for what he puts up with from the Frost household."

"What's that? Table scraps and more belly rubs than he can handle?" Marissa guessed.

Zach let out a loud laugh. "Yeah. That and being locked up in the house, unable to terrorize the Christmas tree farm customers for an entire month. He's not much of a fan of that."

"Can't say I blame him." Marissa ran her hand down Pumpkin's back. "I wouldn't want to be cooped up either. Although I do thank my lucky stars that Pumpkin's idea of a perfect day is to cuddle up by the fire."

"Wouldn't that be nice," he said, sounding wistful. "Though he is a great hiking partner, I'll give him that."

"Here Comes Santa Claus" started to play over the loudspeakers, and Zach said, "Time to roll." Then he looked at his dog and added, "Don't chase the snowmen this year. If you do, they'll ban us for good. Understand?"

Spruce ignored the question and bounded back into the cart, eager to get the show on the road.

"He chased the snowmen last year?" Danny asked.

Marissa laughed. "Yep. They walk the parade and dance when the music plays. Spruce decided he didn't like their dance moves and chased one up the giant tree in the middle of the square last year. It was the talk of the town for days afterward. He's kind of a legend."

"Wow." Danny looked at Pumpkin. "Don't embarrass your mother like that, okay? We're more respectable than that."

Pumpkin let out a little yip that he interpreted to mean she most definitely would not be chasing anything.

Twenty minutes later, he found out he couldn't have been more wrong.

CHAPTER 21

*M*arissa loved the Paw-mas parade. It was something she looked forward to every year. Christmas and puppies. What could be better? Usually she and Pumpkin walked it, so this year was a little different with the golf cart. But she had to admit that it didn't suck. Since she didn't have to make sure Pumpkin didn't get tangled in the crowd, it was easier to see everything.

The moment they rolled past the starting point, the cart was suddenly flanked by life-sized Saint Bernard nutcrackers. They marched along, in perfect formation, only peeling off to make room for poodle ballet dancers that twirled in their pink tutus.

Pumpkin sat on Danny's lap, perfectly still and at attention as she took in the spectacle. When the bulldogs on hogs showed up twirling their candy cane batons, her tail started to wag uncontrollably, and Marissa got the impression that her little Havanese pup had a bit of a bad boy streak.

"This is incredible," Danny said, his eyes wide. "Christmas Grove really knows how to put on a parade."

"They really do," she said with a nod, feeling happier and more at ease than she had in weeks. The stress of the accident and the curse seemed to fade away as she let herself just enjoy the moment.

One of the bulldogs on hogs rode up next to them. The woman driving the motorcycle grinned at Danny as Pumpkin barked her enthusiasm, clearly ready to jump aboard. Marissa wasn't sure if she was more excited about the motorcycle or the bulldog in the side car who was making eyes at her.

"I hate to be the heavy, Pumpkin," Marissa said. "But I seriously doubt there will be any motorcycles in your future."

Her dog turned and gave her an evil puppy glare and then went back to wagging her tail for the bulldog.

Danny laughed as he held on to Pumpkin, making sure she didn't run off with the leather-clad stud.

"Am I hearing what I think I'm hearing?" Danny asked as they got close to a set of bleachers on the left.

"Are you talking about the dog choir?" she asked.

"Yes! Are they barking 'Jingle Bells'?"

"Yep." She glanced ahead at the stands full of dogs and their humans. The mishmash of dog breeds were all wearing Santa hats and standing at attention as they barked out the song. "They're pretty good, right?"

"Now I've seen it all. A dog choir," he said, shaking his head, clearly amused.

"Hardly." She leaned over and gave him a quick kiss.

Danny placed one hand on her thigh, and Marissa just felt right. No matter what else was going on, she knew she'd made the right choice by letting Danny back into her life.

Snow started to fall over the parade just as a pack of huskies appeared, pulling Santa and his sleigh. Santa made snowballs from the falling snow and started throwing them to the pups lined up watching the parade. Their humans cackled at the way the snowballs melted, leaving the dogs confused as to where their balls had gone.

Pumpkin watched the confused dogs with a look of superiority that made Marissa chuckle. "You're smarter than that, aren't you, girl?"

Pumpkin glanced at her and opened her mouth in a big doggie grin.

"What is that?" Danny asked, leaning out of the cart as he looked ahead.

"What?" Marissa bent her head, trying to see past the top of the golf cart and then frowned. "Why is the snow princess wearing black?"

Every year, the parade ended up pausing at the crowned snow princess who gave out holiday treats to all the dogs. She was usually dressed in a white gown and wore a crown made of ice. This year, the princess was in a lacey black dress, black boots, and was wearing a black eye mask that made her look more like she was going to a masquerade ball. Plus, there weren't any treats in sight. Instead, she had a silver wand with a red star at the end and was writing something in the air that Marissa couldn't quite make out.

"What does that say?" Danny asked, squinting.

The words kept erasing and reappearing.

"I think it says *No barking*," Marissa said. The words disappeared and the queen wrote, *Stay off the couch!* "Who hired this grump?"

There were boos behind them from the group that was walking their golden retrievers.

Marissa turned and gave them a thumbs-up.

Just as they started to pass the Cruella queen, the words changed and all hell broke loose.

No dogs allowed!

Pumpkin started to growl, baring her teeth, and then she jerked violently from Danny's grip and shot out of the cart, heading straight for the queen.

"Pumpkin! No!" Marissa darted after her, running as fast as she could, but the little dog was too fast. She had no hope of catching her before she got close enough to attack the queen.

A series of loud barks sounded from behind her, and suddenly Marissa was nearly knocked over when Spruce darted past her, ornaments flying off him left and right.

"Dammit, Spruce! I warned you about this," Zach called, now racing after the dogs, too.

While Pumpkin darted between legs and skirted around most of the parade-goers with ease, Spruce was busy knocking people over in his haste to go after Cruella. Pumpkin reached Cruella first, grabbing onto the black lace skirt and yanking with everything she had. The queen scowled at the dog, pointed her wand at her, and sent a crackle of magic that made Marissa's heart stop.

"No!" Marissa cried just as Spruce threw himself in front of the magic, saving Pumpkin from the electric blow. Spruce let out a loud wince and then dropped right in front of Pumpkin, whimpering and twitching from the magic.

"What the actual hell?" Marissa cried as she threw herself at the queen, grabbing the wand and trying to yank it out of her hand. "How dare you attack our dogs like that. You could have killed one of them!"

The queen pulled back out of Marissa's grasp and managed to not only keep the wand, but tore her skirt away from the furious Pumpkin, who clearly wanted to rip it to shreds.

Zach reached them and fell to his knees beside Spruce. He ran a hand down his flank, talking calmly to his dog, trying to soothe him.

"You're blaming me?" the woman asked. Her voice was vaguely familiar. "Your dog attacked me. What was I supposed to do? Let her rip my leg off?"

Marissa reached for her snarling dog and held her close, trying to calm her. Both of them were shaking, and Marissa was beside herself. Pumpkin had never attacked anyone in her life. In her five-plus years, she hadn't been anything but sweet to everyone she'd ever known.

"What have you done to my dog?" Zach yelled as he got to his feet, fuming at the woman. "He didn't do anything to you. Just look at him."

Marissa followed his gaze and saw that poor Spruce was having trouble standing on all four paws. He'd gotten up but was holding his front left paw up, wincing when he tried to put any weight on it.

"You don't belong here," Marissa seethed at her. "This is a dog parade to celebrate them, not use magic to hurt them!"

"Patience!" Sophie cried as she appeared out of nowhere right next to Cruella. "You don't belong here!" She waved a hand, removing the woman's mask.

Marissa let out a gasp when she realized why the woman's voice was familiar. She was Sophie's sister, the fallen sugar plum fairy who'd cursed Danny and threatened her the night of his accident. "You! What are you *doing* here?"

"Wreaking havoc like she always does," Sophie spat. "What are you trying to do? Sabotage my bid for my wings? I know you don't care about Danny or that curse you cast sixteen years ago. If you did, you'd have tried to stick your claws into him well before now. Admit it! You're jealous of me!"

Marissa clutched Pumpkin and took a few steps back away from the two sugar plum fairies. Magic was sparking off Sophie like a live wire, and she didn't want either of them in the way of whatever was about to transpire. "Zach," she whispered, "we need to move."

Zach hauled Spruce into his arms and the pair of them turned to hurry back to the golf carts, but Marissa stopped short when she found Danny standing right behind her, leaning on his crutches.

"Danny, what are you doing?" she asked, wanting to pull him back to the golf carts.

"Protecting my girls," he said, glaring at Patience. "She already cost me years with you. I won't let it happen again."

"Danny, hey man. I don't think we want to get involved in whatever this is," Zach said, trying to be the voice of reason.

But Danny shook him off. "You don't understand. This evil fairy cursed me. I'm not running again. Not now. Not ever."

Marissa felt tears sting her eyes as emotion overtook her. She turned to face the woman who'd destroyed their lives and grabbed Danny's hand, holding on as tightly as she could while still clutching Pumpkin. "I'm not running either!" she called.

Danny met her gaze. "I didn't think there was ever any question of that."

She wanted to confirm that he was speaking the truth, but she couldn't. Because ever since Patience appeared to her in the hospital after his accident, she'd been wondering if Danny had made the right choice all those years ago. Wondered if the only way to keep him safe was to keep her distance.

"Marissa?" he asked with concern etched in the lines around his eyes.

"She came to me. After your accident. Told me she'd never leave us alone," she blurted. "I kept wondering if maybe we should end this before we get in any deeper."

"Is that what you want?" he asked and then looked as if he were holding his breath.

"No. It isn't. But I finally understood why you left. After seeing you hurt like that..." She shook her head, trying to dislodge the emotion from her throat. "I don't ever want to see you hurting again. I thought... I don't know. If it was the only way to keep you safe, I'd go. I'd keep my distance. Even leave this town if that's what it took. I love you too much to put you in danger."

Tears were rolling down her cheeks unchecked.

Danny reached over and brushed them away. "But I was wrong to leave. I should have stayed and fought for you. I'm prepared to do that now. I pray that you are willing to do the same."

It seemed as if everyone around them was holding their breath, waiting to see how their drama played out.

Marissa looked around at the expectant faces and then up at Patience, who was scowling at them.

The evil fairy said, "I'll never be far away. You'll always be looking over your shoulder, waiting to see what I have in store for you both. Leave him now. It's the only way to save yourself."

The words sparked a fire in Marissa, and she knew then that she'd never stop fighting for Danny. He was her soulmate. The one she'd loved since she was barely a teenager. The one she'd never stopped loving. And the one she'd die waiting for if she didn't make this choice right at that moment. "Nothing you say or do will ever come between us. Danny is mine. And I'm his." She turned back to him. "I love you. She can't do anything to change that. If you're in this with me, then I'm in, too. All in. Forever."

Relief shone in his green eyes as he clutched her and Pumpkin to him. "I'm yours, Marissa Cane. Never again will I let anyone get between us."

Magic sparked around them, swirling in a shimmering light. It tickled Marissa's arms, filled her up, and made her feel invincible. She laughed up at Danny as he smiled down at her, and then suddenly all that magic shot upward, gathered into the shape of a broken heart, and then burst like fireworks on the 4th of July.

"No!" Patience cried right at the same moment that Sophie let out an excited squeal as she twirled around, showing off her new wings.

The translucent wings were almost twice her size, and when she fluttered them, she lifted right off the ground.

"Whoa," Zach said.

"This is the best Paw-mas parade this town has ever had!" someone shouted from behind them.

People started chattering, and the music started up again as if nothing had ever happened. Zach took Spruce back to his golf cart where they waited for the parade to start up again.

But Marissa didn't move. She was too transfixed. Four other fairies appeared out of nowhere, each of them with wings just like Sophie's. Together, the five of them circled Patience, grabbing her by her tacky black lace dress and carrying her away from the parade.

"What do you think they'll do with her?" Danny asked.

"I have no idea. Maybe Sophie will come back some

time to give us an update." She leaned into him, grateful for his solid presence. "Do you feel any different?"

"I feel lighter. Like a weight or fog has been lifted. I don't know, it's like I've been carrying a physical burden for so many years I was just used to it. But now I feel like I'm on top of the world. What about you?"

She gave him a sweet smile and said, "I feel like a piece of myself was just returned to me. And I don't care about being on top of the world, just as long as I have you."

"You have me. Always." Then he dipped his head and kissed her.

A loud chorus of horns honking overpowered the music and general din of the crowd.

Marissa pulled away from Danny and glanced over to see a dozen golf carts all pulled up behind the one they'd abandoned. She chuckled. "I think it's time to rejoin the parade."

Together, the three of them made their way back to the golf cart and then took off, eager to rejoin the festivities.

"Do you think we'll meet Santa?" Danny asked.

"I'm hoping for Frosty," Marissa said.

They passed the sleigh that was being pulled by the huskies, and Pumpkin let out a series of barks.

Marissa eyed her pup. "I think that means she wants to meet Rudolph."

Danny threw his head back and laughed, and Marissa knew then and there that they'd finally found their happily-ever-after.

CHAPTER 22

"Merry Christmas Eve," Felicity said as she swept into Sleighed a week later. She was wearing a Santa hat and carrying a plate of Christmas cookies.

"Merry Christmas, everyone!" Clara echoed as she placed her signature fudge on the bar.

"Finally. We've been waiting for you two," Danny said, getting up from his bar stool and using just a cane to walk behind the bar. His ankle was healing well, and he'd already been given a walking cast. He pulled out two identical presents and placed them in front of his girl's two best friends.

Clara raised her eyebrows. "What are these?"

"Christmas presents. What else?" he asked as Marissa came up behind him and then placed two mugs of eggnog on the counter.

"They're from both of us," Marissa said, feeling festive and happier than might be legal. "Sort of. They were my idea, but Danny made them."

"He made them?" Felicity picked the package up and shook it. She frowned when there was no sound or movement.

"Stop that," Clara said. "What if you break it?"

"I'm not gonna break it." Felicity rolled her eyes. But then she sobered and looked at Marissa. "If this is something sappy, I'm going to have to make new friends."

Marissa threw her head back and laughed, but then she wrapped her arms around Danny and leaned into him. Ever since the Paw-mas parade, she and Danny had been inseparable. Well, as inseparable as two people could get when their schedules weren't aligned. She'd been spending her days helping him in the gallery, and he spent most nights hanging out at the pub. Marissa finally felt settled. The roots she'd started to put down in Christmas Grove had really taken hold, and she couldn't wait to see what came next.

Marissa had even confessed to her friends that despite her vow to never get married again, she'd been dreaming about what a real wedding to Danny might look like. She envisioned an outdoor wedding, near a small lake with the mountains as the backdrop. In her dream there was a light dusting of snow, giving the occasion a hint of magic.

She'd been so wistful when she'd spoken about it that Felicity had made a gagging noise and told her that she'd lost her to the dark side. Since then, she'd teased Marissa endlessly about being a lovesick teenager, and all Marissa had done was laugh.

"You can't quit us," Marissa said, grinning at her. "You love us too much."

"That's true," Felicity said grumpily and took a sip of the eggnog. Then she sipped again until the drink was half gone. Once she put the mug down, she added, "Dang, that's good. After the day I had, I needed it."

"Was it crazy at the farm with last minute shoppers?" Marissa asked. Sometimes it was like that on Christmas Eve in Christmas Grove. Though judging by the lack of customers in the pub, she thought most of them were already tucked in at home, waiting for old Saint Nick to arrive.

"No. Not at all," she said, shaking her head. "In fact, I was closing up early when a realtor from Placerville showed up and wanted me to show her around."

"Show her around?" Clara asked, holding one of the Christmas cookies that was decorated like the Grinch. "Show her what?"

"The property. She thought it was for sale."

"What?" Marissa and Clara said at the same time. Marissa cleared her throat. "What made her think that Apples and Spice and Everything Nice was for sale?"

"There's a listing that mentions us, but it's actually the property next door." Felicity rubbed at her forehead. "It's owned by my estranged aunt. The one my father cut out of his life thirty years ago." She fingered the rim of her mug. "I tried to get in touch with her about buying it, but there's no number, and the listing agent said she's not interested in selling to the family."

Marissa's eyes went wide when she asked, "Why in the world not?"

"I have no idea. And there's no one to ask, either." There was frustration in her tone when she added, "I knew she and my dad had a falling out years ago, but I had no idea it was this bad. I don't even think she knows he passed on."

Clara covered Felicity's hand with hers and squeezed. "I'm sorry, Felicity. That's not exactly the kind of news one should be getting at Christmas."

"No, it's not. Especially since the company that wants to buy it is interested in developing condos," she spat out. "I guess I know what I'm doing with my new year. Fighting commercial development in Christmas Grove." She raised her mug and waited for them all to toast.

"We'll help," Marissa said, unable to imagine condos invading the lovely apple orchards of Christmas Grove.

"We'll do whatever we can," Clara added.

"I know." Felicity smiled at them gratefully. "The farm, that land, it's the only thing that really means anything to me, and the idea of seeing condos where my grandmother's magical garden used to be just makes me shudder with disgust."

"I bet it does." Marissa knew that Felicity walked the path to her grandmother's cabin regularly. They'd been very close right up until the very end when Felicity had been holding her hand as her grandmother took her last breath. She'd lived well into her nineties and had lived a rich life, but it was a loss that had affected Felicity deeply. It was the reason she lived in town with Clara. Living on the farm without her grandmother had just been too hard. "We won't let it happen," Marissa promised. "One way or another, we'll find a way to keep it as it should be."

"Thanks." Felicity looked down at the package that was still on the bar. "Enough of my woes. Should we open these now?"

"Yes," Marissa said, knowing it would cheer her up.

"Together?" Felicity asked Clara.

"Definitely."

The pair raced to rip the Christmas paper free of the small cardboard boxes and then were careful to open the flaps at the same time.

And once they pulled the matching mugs out and held them up, both of them burst out laughing.

Felicity's was a deep red with a silhouette of a woman leaning against a door emblazoned with the words *Looking for Mr. Right Now*, while Clara's was pink with an engraved heart that read *Looking for Mr. Right*.

"Oh. Em. Gee. These are perfect," Clara said with a snort. "I love mine."

Felicity chuckled. "I love mine, too. It'll be a warning sign for anyone I bring home. They won't get any ideas about forever."

They all laughed and then spent the next few hours enjoying the nog and snacking on fudge and Christmas cookies.

As the sun started to go down, Danny glanced at his phone. "Time to close up. We have somewhere to be."

"We do?" all three of the women said.

Then Clara said, "Oh, right. You two have somewhere to be. Felicity and I just have a date with the Christmas Movie Channel."

"Speak for yourself," Felicity said as Jackson walked into the pub, looking like he'd just stepped out of a *Mountain Men* magazine. He was wearing a flannel shirt, clean jeans that showed off his rounded backside, and had a soft red scarf around his neck. Felicity smiled at him as she added, "I have a date with an actual human, thank you very much."

"You do?" Clara and Marissa asked at the same time.

"She does," Jackson said, holding his hand out for her. "I promised her a snowshoeing trip under the moonlight."

"You're going snowshoeing?" Clara asked her, blinking in confusion.

"I snowshoe," she said defensively. "I did grow up on a farm, remember?"

"Sure, but the last time you went on a hike you—"

"Never mind that," Felicity said, cutting her off. "Let's go, Jackson. I can't think of a better way to spend Christmas Eve." She turned toward her friends. "Are we still on for breakfast?"

Danny nodded. "Yep. Waffles and bacon. Be there to be merry."

She groaned. "Never say that again."

They all laughed and watched as Felicity left on her date with Jackson. When the door shut, Clara said, "That's my cue. You lovebirds have fun, okay?"

"Wait." Marissa put a hand on her arm. "Are you really going home to watch movies by yourself?"

She smiled softly. "I'm going home to enjoy a nice long bath and start a new book I got for myself. Tomorrow we'll do Christmas up right. Now let me go before my new book boyfriend invades someone else's bath."

She hopped off the stool and waved as she hurried out of the pub.

"Was that a little strange?" she asked Danny.

He shook his head. "No. They know I have something special planned."

Before they could make their escape, the door swung open and Sophie walked in. Her head was held high as she fluttered her wings, looking impressive against the holiday lights that framed the door. "Merry Christmas Eve," she said, her eyes twinkling. "I trust your days have been much less exciting since the last time I saw you."

"You'd be correct," Marissa said. "Nothing heavy has tried to fall on me or run me over since the Paw-mas parade. I believe I have you to thank for that."

"You can thank yourselves," she said, beaming. "It's because you and Danny stood up for yourselves and believed in each other that *you* broke the curse. It's me who should be thanking you. And apologizing. It turns out that Patience did cast that curse because she wanted Danny, but the moment he ran from you the first time, she lost interest and went after someone else. She was only back here because she didn't want me to get my wings."

"But you did anyway. Congratulations," Danny said.

"And thank you for explaining what was happening. Without that, I'm not sure Marissa and I would be here."

"It was nothing," she said, giving them a wide smile. "Okay, it was something. I'm just glad it worked out."

Marissa cleared her throat. "I saw you and some other sugar plum fairies carrying her off. What happened to her?"

"Rehab for fairies gone bad." Sophie shuddered. "If she graduates, they'll let her reenter society on a trial basis. If she doesn't, then she'll be stuck at the fairy compound, destined to serve the powers that be."

"That's... bleak," Marissa said.

"It's what she deserves," Sophie said. "Sugar plum fairies are supposed to bring joy, not devastation. And that is exactly why I'm here." She smiled and sprinkled a bit of magic in the air. It swirled around and then formed a small gold locket that glowed with magic. "It's a talisman for your home. Hang it over your front door, and your love will be protected for all your days to come."

The locket moved until it was right in front of Marissa.

"Hold out your hand," Sophie said.

Marissa did as she was told, and when the locket fell gently into her palm, a calmness settled over her, making her feel grounded and as if life had never been sweeter.

"Wherever you end up, as long as you're together, this locket will watch over you. If there's ever a time you need a little sugar plum fairy magic, just call me and I'll hear you." Sophie kissed them both on the cheek and then disappeared into the ether.

"That was kind," Danny said.

"It was, but I hope we never need this," she said, slipping the locket into her purse.

"Agreed." He nodded and then tugged gently on her hand. "Let's get going before it gets much colder out."

She raised her eyebrows. "What do you have planned, Danny Frost?"

"You'll see."

CHAPTER 23

"*A* romantic evening with Pumpkin?" Marissa asked Danny as he slid back into his brand new 4Runner after stopping at Marissa's to pick up her dog. His old SUV had been totaled, and thanks to insurance, he been able to get a new one with all the bells and whistles.

He glanced at her and laughed. "I said it was a surprise, not a romantic evening."

"But there's wine and a picnic basket in the back seat. What am I supposed to think?" she asked.

"That I have a surprise for you... and Pumpkin." Danny smirked at her.

"You're the worst." She sat back in the seat, her arms crossed over her chest as she pretended to be annoyed. But when Pumpkin nudged her with her nose, Marissa relented and tugged the happy creature into her lap. "Just a couple of kisses and then into your car bed. Understand?"

Pumpkin licked Marissa's face twice and then laid down in her lap.

Marissa chuckled to herself, knowing her dog would be quite content to ride right there, but Marissa wasn't taking any chances. She took a moment to get Pumpkin settled in her car bed in the back seat, and once Marissa was back in her own seat and buckled up, she said, "Okay. I'm ready to be dazzled."

"I'm just the man for the challenge," he said and put the vehicle in gear.

MARISSA STARED out the window of the 4Runner at the scene in front of her, speechless. Hundreds of luminary bags were lit up on the otherwise empty property, shaped in what appeared to be the outline of a house.

"Danny?" she asked, her voice barely a whisper.

"Come on, love. I want to show you what I've been planning." He slipped out of the 4Runner and hobbled around to her side of the vehicle. By the time he got there, Marissa had already freed Pumpkin from her travel bed and was waiting with her hand out.

He took it and kissed the back of her hand. "Someday soon, I'm going to be fast enough to be opening doors for you again."

She chuckled. "I'm sure you will."

Pumpkin stayed right at their feet, despite the fact that there wasn't a fence or anything to keep her from exploring the area.

"You're just as curious as I am, aren't you, little girl?" Marissa said to her.

Pumpkin looked up and wagged her tail, giving her confirmation.

Danny took Marissa by the hand and led her over to the luminary lights. "You already know that I rent the barn apartment on the farm next door."

She nodded. "Sure. This isn't part of their land?"

He shook his head. "No. When I moved to Christmas Grove, my plan was to buy a place, but when I couldn't find anything remotely suitable, I decided to buy land. A place to build my forever home." He waved a hand at the acreage in front of them. "This is the land I chose."

"You own this?" she asked, shocked. She'd had no idea that he'd put down roots that deep in Christmas Grove. She knew he owned his gallery and adjoining studio, but in a town like Christmas Grove, those could always be sold or rented out fairly easily if things didn't work out.

"I do. The reason I rent the apartment next door is because I met the owner one day while I was contemplating where to put a fifth wheel while I built something, and he offered the apartment to me. It was an easy decision. And since then, I've been trying to decide what type of house to put here. Now it seems important that I ask you that same question."

She let out a soft chuckle. "It's not my house, Danny. Why would you ask me?"

He smiled down at her and said, "I'm hoping to change that."

"What?" She blinked at him.

"This way." He nudged her forward, and together they walked carefully toward the lighted display. When he stepped over the first row of lights, he picked up Pumpkin and gestured for Marissa to join him.

"What are we doing?" she asked with a nervous chuckle.

He set Pumpkin back down and took both her hands in his. "A few weeks ago, before all the stuff with Sophie and her sister started, I had a dream about this house. Right where we're standing is where the swing was on the porch. We were sitting here in the early morning, enjoying the crisp air and view of the mountains. It was heaven. You and me together. Forever."

"It sounds like heaven to me," she said, her heart suddenly trying to beat right out of her chest.

"I wanted it to be one of my visions." He gave her a wan smile. "I didn't think that was possible, since we both know that I never dream my visions. They just come on out of nowhere. But there are two things that make me think that maybe, just maybe, this time my dream might become a reality."

Her throat was dry when she forced out, "What two things?"

He glanced at Pumpkin. "This little one, who I hadn't even met yet, came bouncing out of the house to sit with us. You called her Pumpkin in my dream."

Marissa sucked in a sharp breath, suddenly feeling awash in the love he had for her. Her head swam as emotions overwhelmed her, the emotions she hadn't felt from him in over sixteen years. "And the second thing?"

"You also called me Mr. Garland. At the time, I thought for sure it was just a weird dream thing, but then—"

"You won Mr. Garland at the Christmas Tree Festival," she finished for him as a laugh bubbled up from the depths of her soul.

He nodded. "Exactly. So here I am, hoping that the rest of my dream becomes a reality."

"But I don't understand. How did you see all that in your dream?" she asked. "Are your powers changing?"

"Maybe. But if they are, it's because of you. I told you years ago that you bewitched me. I don't think that's ever changed."

"You always did call me your little witch," she said, pressing her hand to his cheek.

Using his cane, Danny very carefully lowered himself so that he was kneeling on one knee. Then he pulled the small velvet box out of his pocket and opened it, revealing a large round diamond ring. "Marissa Cane, my little witch, will you do me the honor of being my wife? Only this time, no matter what comes our way, it's forever."

She stared down at him with tear-filled blurry eyes and then looked up at the lights all around them and the shadowy mountains in the distance. Her heart calmed, and when she met his gaze again, this time with clear eyes, she smiled softly and said, "Yes."

Danny let out a long breath, labored to his feet, and then crushed her in a hug, holding on so tight she would have laughed if she was able. She nudged him gently, sucked in some air, and said, "Okay, show me our house."

He grinned. "It's a farmhouse, just like we always used to talk about. You're gonna love it."

CHAPTER 24

$\mathscr{F}$elicity Hill sped down the two-lane road that led to her bestie's new house and prayed she made it on time. Of all the days to have an emergency at the farm, today was not the day.

The Christmas season was always stressful at Apples and Spice and Everything Nice, her family farm that she'd taken over running just six years prior. But that was mostly because it was the last month of their busy season. So when she woke up to a frantic message that the point-of-sale system was down and they couldn't take credit cards, she'd jumped in her Jeep and headed straight for the office.

An hour later, after dealing with IT over the phone, the system was once again working, and she was dangerously late.

Just as she turned into the long driveway that led to the gorgeous farmhouse, a little snow began to fall.

Felicity's cold dead heart melted. She knew Marissa had been hoping for a blanket of snow on her wedding day. And just like that, as if she'd spelled it into existence, the snow was right on time.

Felicity pulled up beside the familiar Ford F150 that she knew belonged to Jackson and jumped out of her Jeep. After grabbing her sparkling heels, she ran into the house. "I'm here. I made it!"

"It's about time," Clara said with a huff. "I know you're not a romantic, but come on, City. It's your best friend's wedding. Sitting this one out isn't an option."

Felicity bit back an annoyed retort. There was no way on the goddess's green earth that she'd miss this. She might not be into marriage and weddings, but that didn't mean she wouldn't show up for her besties. "I'm here, aren't I?"

Clara looked up from the mirror and grimaced at her friend. "Sit," she ordered. "Your hair looks like you've been through a wind tunnel."

Felicity glanced in the mirror and patted it down. "It doesn't look that bad." Though Clara had a point. Her hair could use a practiced hand. "I was on the verge of tearing it out when I got called in to deal with IT this morning."

"That's where you were?" Clara asked, looking remorseful. "Sorry. When you weren't at the house this morning, I assumed you'd stayed over with your mystery man last night."

Felicity rolled her eyes. "I left you a note. Didn't you see it?"

"No. Crap, where was it?"

"On the fridge. I figured you'd see it when you got coffee."

Clara frowned. "I might have been a little late myself. I stopped in town for coffee." After a few swipes of a brush and a couple of fancy twists, Clara put Felicity's hair into shape, making it look like she'd gone to a professional. "There. Now you're ready for pictures."

"Damn. You're good. If the glassblowing ever goes south, you could open your own salon," Felicity said.

"Please don't wish that on me," Clara said with a laugh. "Now come on. We don't want to make them wait any longer."

The pair of them walked out to the back where a handful of guests were seated. Danny and Jackson were already at the altar, waiting for the wedding to start.

"You're here. Thank the gods. The officiant is getting impatient," Marissa said. "I don't think she likes the snow."

Felicity focused on the woman who was standing near Danny and laughed. It was Sophie, the sugar plum fairy, and she kept fluttering her wings to keep the snow from accumulating on them. "Somehow, I think that's fitting."

"Me, too." Marissa beamed. Then she nodded to the DJ, who started the music.

"You Make it Feel Like Christmas" by Gwen Stefani and Blake Shelton started to play, and the next thing Felicity knew, Marissa was promising to spend the rest of her days with the love of her life.

Felicity discreetly wiped the lone tear that fell when Marissa said I do, and then she thanked the goddess that Clara was too busy mopping up her own face to notice.

The last thing she needed was for her friends to find out that she really did have at least one sentimental bone in her body.

What she wasn't counting on was for Jackson Bell to be watching. And when their eyes met, he tapped his ring finger and mouthed, *You're next.*

DEANNA'S BOOK LIST

<u>Witches of Keating Hollow:</u>
Soul of the Witch
Heart of the Witch
Spirit of the Witch
Dreams of the Witch
Courage of the Witch
Love of the Witch
Power of the Witch
Essence of the Witch
Muse of the Witch
Vision of the Witch
Waking of the Witch
Honor of the Witch
Promise of the Witch
Return of the Witch
Fortune of the Witch

Song of the Witch
Rise of the Witch

Witches of Befana Bay:
The Witch's Silver Lining
The Witch's Secret Love
The Witch's Lost Spell

Witches of Christmas Grove:
A Witch For Mr. Holiday
A Witch For Mr. Christmas
A Witch For Mr. Winter
A Witch For Mr. Mistletoe
A Witch For Mr. Frost
A Witch For Mr. Garland
A Witch For Mr. Bell

Premonition Pointe Novels:
Witching For Grace
Witching For Hope
Witching For Joy
Witching For Clarity
Witching For Moxie
Witching For Kismet

Miss Matched Midlife Dating Agency:
Star-crossed Witch
Honor-bound Witch
Outmatched Witch
Moonstruck Witch

Rainmaker Witch

Jade Calhoun Novels:
Haunted on Bourbon Street
Witches of Bourbon Street
Demons of Bourbon Street
Angels of Bourbon Street
Shadows of Bourbon Street
Incubus of Bourbon Street
Bewitched on Bourbon Street
Hexed on Bourbon Street
Dragons of Bourbon Street

Pyper Rayne Novels:
Spirits, Stilettos, and a Silver Bustier
Spirits, Rock Stars, and a Midnight Chocolate Bar
Spirits, Beignets, and a Bayou Biker Gang
Spirits, Diamonds, and a Drive-thru Daiquiri Stand
Spirits, Spells, and Wedding Bells

Ida May Chronicles:
Witched To Death
Witch, Please
Stop Your Witchin'

Crescent City Fae Novels:
Influential Magic
Irresistible Magic
Intoxicating Magic

Last Witch Standing:
Bewitched by Moonlight
Soulless at Sunset
Bloodlust By Midnight
Bitten At Daybreak

Witch Island Brides:
The Wolf's New Year Bride
The Vampire's Last Dance
The Warlock's Enchanted Kiss
The Shifter's First Bite

Destiny Novels:
Defining Destiny
Accepting Fate

Wolves of the Rising Sun:
Jace
Aiden
Luc
Craved
Silas
Darien
Wren

Black Bear Outlaws:
Cyrus
Chase
Cole

<u>Bayou Springs Alien Mail Order Brides:</u>

Zeke

Gunn

Echo

ABOUT THE AUTHOR

New York Times and USA Today bestselling author, Deanna Chase, is a native Californian, transplanted to the slower paced lifestyle of southeastern Louisiana. When she isn't writing, she is often goofing off with her husband in New Orleans or playing with her two shih tzu dogs. For more information and updates on newest releases visit her website at deannachase.com.